Alexis has always been the wild child. She's the girl everyone always gossips about behind her back. Now that she's engaged to the town's bad boy, Travis, she finally thinks she's heading in the right direction. Then life throws a tall, dark, and good man her way and causes her whole world to shake.

Grant's back in town. Helping his father with his legal practice had never been in his plan. But after trying to live in the city and deciding it wasn't for him, he wants nothing more than to settle back down in his hometown. He even buys a small farm to prove to himself that he's back to stay. After stepping in and helping the town's bad girl out one night, he starts to see beneath Alexis' act. Now all he needs to do is convince her that choosing a good guy is not always a bad thing.

Table of Contents

Other titles by Jill Sanders

The Pride Series
Finding Pride – Pride Series #1
Discovering Pride – Pride Series #2
Returning Pride – Pride Series #3
Lasting Pride – Pride Series #4
Serving Pride – Prequel to Pride Series #5
Red Hot Christmas – A Pride Christmas #6
My Sweet Valentine – Pride Series #7

The Secret Series
Secret Seduction – Secret Series #1
Secret Pleasure – Secret Series #2
Secret Guardian – Secret Series #3
Secret Passions – Secret Series #4
Secret Identity – Secret Series #5
Secret Sauce – Secret Series #6

The West Series
Loving Lauren – West Series #1
Taming Alex – West Series #2
Holding Haley – West Series #3

This is a work of fiction. Names, characters, places and incidents either are the product of the author's imagination or are used fictitiously, and any resemblance to actual persons, living or dead, business establishments, events or locales is entirely coincidental.

ISBN: 978-1497415362
Copyright © 2014 Jill Sanders
Editor: Erica Ellis – www.ericaellisfreelance.com

Taming Alex

by
Jill Sanders

Jill Sanders

Dedication

To all those good girls
out there
with a secret wild side…

Jill Sanders

Prologue

Alex stood in the grocery store. She looked up and down the aisles before slipping the small figurine into her coat pocket. Oh, she knew that stealing was wrong, but since God had taken away her mother a few months ago, she figured He owed her one. Besides, her ma had promised to buy the small horse for her on her seventh birthday. That day had come and gone last week. She'd prayed and prayed that her mother would get her the small metal horse from heaven somehow, but after she'd opened the last of her presents at her small birthday party and there was still no horse, she'd known exactly what she needed to do.

It was the first day of school, and she'd convinced Lauren to walk with her to the Grocery Stop after school. The Grocery Stop was Fairplay's only market, and was only a few blocks from their school. They had a whole hour to wait for their pa before he'd be able to come and pick them up.

Getting her sister to leave her alone in the aisle where the small statues sat in a large glass case took a lot of talking. Finally, Alex had told her big sister that she had to use the bathroom. When Lauren wanted to come into the small room with her, Alex had thrown a fit.

"I'm a big girl. I don't want you watching me." She'd stood there with her hands on her hips, just like their ma used to do. Her sister finally told her that she'd wait for her at the front counter and left her alone. She waited in the bathroom long enough so that her sister could make it up front. Then she peeked out the crack of the door to make sure that she had disappeared. She tiptoed down the aisle and pocketed the horse smoothly. She hadn't counted on a hand dropping onto her shoulder.

"You aren't supposed to do that."

Alex spun around to see Grant "Do-gooder" Holton standing behind her. Grant was the same age as Alex and had earned the nickname by being the town's biggest tattletale. He thought that just because his daddy was the town's hotshot lawyer that he had to tell everyone else what to do. All the other kids at school made fun of him about it.

Grant was a little taller than she was. Then again, almost everyone was taller than she was. Her mother had said that she was a small statue. Alex didn't know what that meant, but she wasn't happy that Haley, her little sister, was already taller than she was.

She looked across the aisle at Grant. He was chubby and wore glasses that were always sliding off his nose. He was always wearing his best church clothes, or so Alexis always thought, since she'd never seen him in a pair of jeans or a T-shirt, ever. His hair always looked like he had just combed it, and she had never seen him dirty.

Alex thought the glasses made him look smarter and desperately wished that she needed glasses so she would do better in math class, but the doctor had said she had perfect eyes. Grant's hair was a shade darker than her own blonde, but his had a curl to it. She wished she had curly hair, since her hair was so thin it was hard to braid.

She wrapped her small fingers around the cool metal of the horse in her pocket. "I'm not giving it back." She stomped her foot. "God owes it to me since he took my mama away." Her eyes started to water up and her bottom lip quivered.

"Stealing is a sin. Besides, you can go to jail if they catch you." His face started turning a darker shade of red. "I'm gonna have to tell."

She reached out and grabbed his coat before he could walk away. "Don't you dare, Grant Holton." She looked up at him and thought of a way out of this mess. "If...if you promise not to tell anyone..." Her little mind desperately reached for some means to hold him to a promise. "I promise..." He waited, his big blue eyes looking into hers, and she blurted out. "I'll let you kiss me."

Grant's eyes got bigger behind his glasses. He thought about it a moment, then said, "For real?" He looked around.

What was it to her? She'd seen her ma and pa do it lots of times. She didn't see what all the fuss was about, since it looked sloppy and gross, but if it got Grant to shut up about the statue, she'd tolerate it.

She nodded her head her eyes and smiled.

"Sure."

"On the lips?" His head tilted as he waited.

"Why not? Is it a deal?"

Grant thought about it for another second, then nodded his head as he pushed up his glasses. When he took a step closer to her, she almost lost her nerve. Instead, she closed her eyes and puckered up her lips like she'd seen her mother do. When his lips touched hers she wanted to pull back and wipe her mouth off, but then something happened. She started to like it. His lips were soft and not wet, after all. They felt like feathers tickling her lips and she actually felt her feet and hands start to tingle.

After what seemed like years, he finally pulled away, a huge smile on his lips. Then he turned and rushed down the aisle and out the front door without a word. She hadn't even made sure he was going to stick to their bargain.

"Come on, Alexis. Dad's here," her sister called from the front of the store.

Smiling, she held onto the small horse in her pocket and walked towards the front. She thought about kissing Grant and decided that she liked kissing. She wanted to do it again and as often as she could. And with as many boys as she wanted to.

Chapter One

Ten years later...

Alex held her breath as her father's coffin was lowered into the ground. Her world was shattered, again. Looking over to Haley, she wondered what would happen to the three of them. After all, Haley was only fourteen. She reached over and grabbed Lauren's hand in her own, then held onto Haley's.

The three of them stood and watched as their father's coffin sank lower into the red dirt at the church's cemetery, in the plot next to their mother's.

Lauren's eyes closed for just a second until her sister dropped her hand and walked over to place a white rose into the hole. It landed softly on the coffin. Lauren turned and nodded to her, then she followed. As she dropped her rose, she stood and said her goodbyes to the man who had done his best to raise the three girls alone and make them

13

happy.

When she turned, Haley walked up and stood next to the hole. Alex couldn't stand it anymore. She turned and walked quickly towards a group of trees. Even though it was spring, the heat was almost too much for her to bear. Here in the shade she could feel the breeze, and she felt like she could finally breathe.

Leaning against the trunk of a large oak tree, she closed her eyes and focused on taking slow breaths. She'd been staying at Cheryl Lynn's house the night that Lauren had found their father on the floor of his room. She should have stayed home that weekend. If she had only stayed...

"Hey." She looked up into Grant's deep blue eyes. He looked pretty much the same as he always had, but his sandy hair was a little longer and he'd gotten new glasses. The wire rims suited his face a little better. He had a slight case of acne on his round face, but his clothes were still spotless.

"Hey." She continued to lean against the tree, crossing her arms over her chest. She started to feel cold and wished for the warmth of the sun again.

"I'm sorry about your dad." He looked down at his shiny boots and kicked a pebble. Grant's father and her father had been best friends since childhood. Even their mothers had been friends, since they'd all grown up in the small town. "I sure hope you don't have to sell your ranch or anything."

Her shoulders came off the tree and she looked at him. "Why would we?" She frowned.

He looked up from his boot and stared at her. "I don't know, I just overheard my pa talking about some money problems your pa had and how Lauren wasn't old enough to take care of you and your sister and a run a ranch at the same time." He raised then dropped his shoulders.

"She's not all by herself. She has Haley and me." She took a step closer to him.

"Well, I hope you're right. I'm leaving at the end of this year. I was accepted into Harvard." He smiled real big.

Her chin dropped and she said, "We're only seventeen."

"I know. I finished all my credits for high school over the summer and my dad and I sent in applications. Can you believe it?" He stuck his hands into his pant pockets.

"You're only seventeen," she repeated.

"Are you gonna miss me?" It came out as a whisper, and Alex didn't hear it. Her mind was stuck on the fact that she was seventeen and now both her parents were gone and she was facing the possibility of losing the only home she'd ever known.

Then she looked over her shoulder and frowned a little. She saw that Grant's father and Mr.

Graham, her father's other best friend, were talking to Lauren next to their truck.

Walking away without saying goodbye, she rushed over to where Haley stood next to her friends and grabbed her hand. "We need to go."

Haley nodded and followed her. They walked up to their sister together.

"We're ready to go home." Alex glared at Mr. Graham and Mr. Holton, who quickly turned their eyes to the ground. Chase, Mr. Graham's son, was standing next to them. He smiled slightly and nodded his head, then the girls left.

The drive home was quiet. Alex wanted to ask her sister what her plans were, but knew it wasn't the right time. Lauren was a week shy of her nineteenth birthday. She was old enough to legally take care of Alex and Haley, that much she knew. She didn't know anything about the money problems their father was having, or even if the ranch had been left to Lauren. Lauren would know all that. After all, for the last few years, Lauren had been helping their father out with the big place.

When the truck turned into their long driveway, Alex looked at their three-story house in the distance. The once freshly painted white building could stand a new coat. The roof had just been replaced a few years back. Alex knew the old place had its problems, but she wouldn't have traded it for any other house in the county.

"Lauren?" She looked at her sister as she

parked the truck, wanting to ask so many questions. Just then, Haley pushed out of the truck and raced towards the barn.

Lauren looked at her and smiled. "I'll get her." Lauren left Alex alone in the truck as she raced after their little sister.

Alex's eyes watered. This was really happening. They were going to lose the ranch. Most likely, they would be split up too. Where were they going to live? What was going to happen to them?

Alex rushed into the house and slowly walked around the place. She was trying to memorize every small detail—all the furnishings, the look and the smell of the place. She ended up in their father's room and when she sat on his bed, she began to softly cry.

It was just like when their mother had died. If she hadn't stopped to grab the cookies, Haley wouldn't have snuck out and run upstairs. Then their mother wouldn't have gone and gotten her. They would have all made it to the shelter in time. Instead, the three girls had had to watch in horror as the tornado ripped their mother into the darkness and out of their lives forever.

If she would have just stayed home this last weekend, their father would still be alive. It was all her fault. Dropping to his bed, she inhaled his rich musky scent and cried until her heart and head hurt. She must have fallen asleep, because when she woke up, it was dark outside the window.

Standing up, she went into her own room and changed into her jeans and work shirt. She knew the horses needed feeding and it had been her job for the last few years. When she walked out to the barn, she saw that the task had already been done. Her shoulders slumped and she sat down in the soft hay, feeling like she'd let her family down again. She made a pact right then and there that she would never let her sisters down again.

Over the course of the next few months, it became apparent that Lauren had everything under control around the ranch. Her sister had even taken over her and Haley's chores, telling them both that they needed to focus on their studies instead.

Lauren had driven Alex down to get her driver's license, and had given her the old red Honda to drive her and Haley to school every day. She didn't mind driving them around all the time, since she knew Lauren was busy. They had sat down the next week and Lauren had told them that all the bills were paid and that no one was going to take the ranch away. Even better, she had signed the official paperwork with Mr. Graham that stated that she had full custody of Alex and Haley. Lauren was their legal guardian. No one was going to separate the three of them, ever.

Alex relaxed into a schedule, knowing that her sister would take care of whatever popped up around the ranch. After a few months, guilt settled in when she noticed how much her sister actually did around the place, and she started doing things without being told to. She asked Jamella down at Mama's for a part-time job and picked up as many hours as she could, just to pay for her gas. But she started making extra money and would always leave it in Lauren's office for her. Her sister never mentioned it, so she continued to give her half of her weekly paycheck. Even Haley picked up on what was going on and started helping out with the animals more and more.

But then just a year later, Alex started dating Travis, and her life had a new purpose—to do everything she could to become Mrs. Travis Nolan.

Almost Eight years later...

Alex stood in the dark parking lot, feeling like kicking something or someone. How could he do this to her again? She looked around the almost-empty lot and felt like screaming.

Instead, she tossed the beer bottle she was holding and smiled when the glass shattered all over his blue truck. The engagement ring on her left finger sparkled in the parking lot's dim lighting. She felt like ripping it off her finger and throwing it as well, but stopped herself before she could follow through. It was her birthday and Travis had gotten so drunk. He was now passed out behind the wheel of his precious truck again. Even the shattering of her beer bottle over his windshield had done little to wake him.

Over the last few months, she'd told herself she was going to really evaluate their relationship. She'd made the decision after Lauren and Chase had sprung it on everyone that they had gotten married the day after their father's funeral. Lauren had married him out of desperation to get out from under a crushing debt, but now they were completely happy about it. Chase had moved into the house and they acted like newlyweds, which she supposed they were since Chase had been gone for the last seven years.

She walked up to Travis' truck and looked at him through his open window. He was still as handsome as the day she'd fallen for him. He had the classic rugged cowboy look that she'd always swooned over. Even the cleft in his chin melted her heart. But lately, his actions were speaking more loudly to her, and she was falling farther and farther away from that soft gooey feeling he had always invoked in her.

She turned and leaned on the truck, crossing her arms over her chest. The steamy, summer night air caused her white blouse to stick to her skin and she desperately wished for a shower. Her hair was plastered to her neck and face, since she and her friends had spent the last few hours line dancing at

The Rusty Rail, the local bar and dance hall. Everyone had come out to celebrate her birthday. A stack of her presents filled the back of Travis' truck. She smiled when she looked back at the packages. Travis had promised her that he wouldn't drink too much tonight, since she hated it when he got so drunk that he started getting rude. He'd never raised a finger towards her, but he did get a little mean with his words and, a few times, she'd had to walk to her friend's house and spend the night instead of letting him drive her home.

"Hey, baby." She turned to see him smiling at her. "Happy birthday." He looked at her funny, then leaned through the window and puked on her white boots.

"Travis!" She jumped back just in time to only get a little splatter.

"Oh, I'm sorry, baby." He started to get out of the truck.

"You're sorry? You've ruined my whole night. You were too busy drinking and hanging out with your buddies to even dance with me." She stepped away from him when he tried to reach over and pull her close. "You forgot to bring my present and, to be honest, I don't think you remembered to get one in the first place."

"I did, honest. It's at my dad's place." She could see the lie in his eyes, which only hurt her more.

"Now you're so drunk you've ruined my favorite boots. Hand me your keys." She held out

21

her hand and tapped her foot. "I'm driving you home, then going home."

He shook his head, then grabbed it and almost toppled over. "No! You know I don't let anyone drive this beauty except me." He tapped his truck and his hand came away wet. "God damn it. Someone's throwing bottles at her." He rushed over and looked at the shattered glass and the almost dry beer.

"I did." She crossed her arms and waited.

"You?" He turned and glared at her. "You scratched her. Why would you do that? It's going to cost hundreds of dollars to buff this out." He was running his fingers over a tiny scratch on the hood. Then he turned towards her with a slight smile on his face. "There goes your birthday present. I'm taking it back to the store so I can pay for this damage."

"Whatever. You know you didn't buy me anything." She started walking away.

"Where are you going? Get back here," he called after her.

"I'm going to Cheryl Lynn's," she called over her shoulder.

"Don't, baby. Come back. I'll give you a ride back to my place." It was an old argument that he had never won. She had never and would never spend the night at his trashed-out apartment over his father's garage. Travis kept the place so dirty, that she'd never even really stepped foot in it. The

22

dirty apartment wasn't the only reason she hadn't spent the night at his place. She couldn't explain it, but she just didn't want to stay there, with him. At least, she talked herself into adding, until they were married.

"Alex, get your butt back here." She knew he'd try a couple different tactics. The next one would be to drive by her and yell at her through the open window. He would start calling her names as she walked, but she always ignored it all, telling herself it was the beer talking.

The next day she would get some flowers and he'd come by and they'd make up. It was their pattern.

But as she walked farther down the dark street towards Cheryl Lynn's place, he didn't drive by her. She turned and looked back at the parking lot and noticed he'd gotten back into the truck.

Probably passed out again, she told herself as she kept walking. Cheryl's place was two miles away, an easy enough walk in the day. But tonight, with the moon only a sliver in the sky, she kept tripping over rocks and clumps of grass along the narrow road.

Less than two minutes later, lights hit her and she stopped and waited until he pulled up next to her. But instead of Travis' truck, a dark black Ford pulled up. When the tinted windows lowered, Grant Holton called out.

"Alexis West is that you? What on earth are you

doing walking along a dark road at this time of night? I could have hit you." It was too dark to see him fully, but she knew that voice anywhere.

"Shut up, Grant." She walked over and pulled open the door to his truck. She was happy when his passenger seat was empty, and she climbed up to sit next to him. "Drive me to Cheryl Lynn's place, would you?" She crossed her arms over her chest and frowned out the front window.

Grant had come home earlier this year and even though the chubby, zit-covered, glasses-wearing geek had been replaced with a skinny, clear-skinned hunk, to her he was the same old Grant "Do-gooder" Holton. Always trying to fix everyone else's problems.

"Travis isn't going to drive you home?" he asked. She turned and glared at him.

"No," she said, then watched as he turned back and looked out the window. He had yet to start driving, and she was slowly getting mad.

"Hmm," he said, and she watched as he looked out the back of his truck towards the Rusty Rail.

"What?" She turned in her seat and glared at him in the dark.

He shook his head. "Nothing."

"Grant Holton, you're lying." Everyone could always tell when he had something to tell. The whole town knew he couldn't hide anything from anyone.

"It's nothing." He reached over and pulled on her seat belt. When his arm brushed against her chest, she held her breath. She knew he hadn't meant the move to mean anything, but still the featherlight touch shocked her.

"Sorry," he mumbled and dropped his arm. "I don't start driving until the seat belts are on."

She rolled her eyes and reached down to finish locking the seat belt into place.

"Are you going to tell me what secret you have?" She looked over at him.

"No secret," he said and then finally put his truck into gear.

"Fine, don't tell me. It's not like I care anyway." She looked out the front window, feeling sad.

"I'm sorry you two broke up on your birthday," he said, causing her head to swivel towards him.

"We didn't break up. Who told you we broke up?" Her voice hitched.

"It's just…I thought…" There was a moment of silence and then he cleared his throat. "I just assumed."

"Why?" She grabbed onto his arm, digging her nails into his skin a little.

He looked over at her, then back towards the road. He remained silent until he pulled the truck off the road into the old train station parking lot.

"When I walked out to leave the Rusty Rail, I

25

saw him and Savannah Douglas making out in the parking lot against his truck." His voice held a hint of sadness, and his eyes, at least what she could see in the darkness, held concern.

"Who put you up to this?" She crossed her arms over her chest again.

"What?" He blinked and leaned back a little. He looked like he was waiting for her to slap him across the face. Instead, she started laughing.

"Oh, this is rich. Did Billy put you up to this?" She stopped chuckling and wiped a tear from her eye. "Billy's always trying to get me to believe that Travis and Savannah have had a thing in the past."

Grant shook his head. "I'm sorry, Alex." He turned and looked out the front window, then was quiet. They sat there for a few seconds before she jumped out of the truck and started quickly walking back to the Rusty Rail.

She heard the truck door slam behind her, then Grant grabbed her shoulders. She swung out, connecting her fist with his chin as tears blinded her eyes.

"That bastard!" she screamed. "He promised it was just a one-time deal." She struck out again, blindly, only connecting with air as his hands wrapped gently around her wrists. "We'd broken up and he was drunk, he said..." She kicked at Grant and tried to get her wrists free, only to be pulled up close against a rock-hard body as muscular arms wrapped around her. Her grief was too much and as the dam behind her eyes finally cut loose, she heard Grant whisper words of kindness into her hair as she cried her heart out against his chest.

Jill Sanders

Chapter Two

Grant held onto Alex and wished with all his heart he could take her hurt away. He knew what he'd seen back at the Rusty Rail. Witnessing the heat between Travis and Savannah, he doubted it had only been a one-time deal.

The rumors had been going around town for months about the relationship, and it was clear that no one was willing to step forward and tell Alex about it. When he'd seen Alex walking along the side of the road, he'd assumed that she already knew about Travis and Savannah back in the parking lot. He couldn't let her walk on a dark road at almost two in the morning all by herself.

Reaching up and running his hand gently down her hair, he wished he hadn't been the one to break the news to her. He should have kept driving and called her sister to come get her. But his parents had raised him to be a better man than that, and he'd been duty bound to stop and pick her up.

The front of his shirt was soaked by the time she finally pulled away and looked up at him. He'd messed up her blonde hair slightly, and he reached up to tuck a strand behind her ear. Her brown eyes softened a little.

"Thank you for being honest with me," she said quietly.

He felt like a dog. He should have lied to her. He should have learned to keep his mouth shut years ago. But when she looked at him with her deep brown eyes, words just spewed from his mouth.

"I'm sorry." He dropped his hand and took a step back.

"Why?" She reached up and twisted her hair until it lay over her shoulder in a twist so it wouldn't fly away in the wind.

"I shouldn't have said anything." He looked down at his boots and wished he could start the night over. It had killed him when he'd shown up at the bar only to see her celebrating her birthday with friends and family, Travis by her side at the table.

Grant had met a few of his friends there for pool, but had spent the rest of the night nursing a beer and watching her dance on the floor with her friends. Ever since that kiss when he was seven, he'd had a thing for her. No other kiss in his long years and many kisses had ever compared to that sweet peck so many years ago. It was the one secret he'd held onto for so many years, and he was probably going to take it to his grave.

"I'm just glad I heard it from a friend first." She looked back towards the Rusty Rail and shivered.

He pulled his light jacket off and placed it over her bare shoulders. Her red rhinestone halter top and cutoff skirt did little to warm her. It was still in the high seventies this late at night, but there was a cool breeze coming from the south.

"You should have a coat," he said as he pulled the jacket closer around her.

"Still trying to fix everyone?" She looked up at him and smiled slightly.

"Only those who need it." He smiled. "Come on, I'll take you home."

"You don't have to. I can stay at…"

"I'll drive you home. You'll want your own bed and your sisters." He waited until she nodded and then turned towards the truck. Opening her door, he helped her step up into the passenger seat.

When he got behind the wheel again, they sat in silence for a while as he drove towards Saddleback Ranch. It wasn't a long drive, but tonight in the darkness and the silence, time seemed to stretch on.

"Why did you come back to Fairplay?" The question threw him for a loop.

31

"Why?" He quickly looked at her.

"Yes. Why come back here? You had your fancy degree from Harvard. You could have opened a law firm anywhere. Why come home?"

"Because it's home." He smiled.

She frowned and turned a little more towards him. "Didn't you want to go places? See foreign cities?"

"I did that for a while." He smiled at her. "I like it better here."

She sighed and turned towards the front again. "I've always wanted to travel. To see Paris in spring. Or spend spring break on some remote Mexican beach."

"Why haven't you?" He looked over at her again and watched her sigh, her shoulders slumping a little.

"Up until a few months ago, I thought I knew the answer. But now…" She looked out the side window and was silent.

"Your sisters?" He turned into the long driveway that led to Saddleback Ranch.

"Yes, one of the reasons." She looked straight ahead at the large white house. Grant had helped Chase and half the men in town put the new metal roof on it a few months ago. He knew that all the windows had been replaced, as well. Chase was in the process of redoing half the house. Since Chase had moved in, officially telling everyone in town about his seven-year marriage to Lauren, he'd been busy fixing the old place up and returning it to its former glory. Or so his friend said. To be honest, Grant couldn't remember the place looking this nice before.

He pulled his truck to a stop in front of the porch and put it into park, leaving it running. "I don't think those reasons are holding you back now."

She looked over at him. "No, I guess I just haven't found the right person to do all that stuff with. I thought…" He saw a tear stream down her cheek and leaned over to gently wipe it away.

"Don't give him your tears. He doesn't deserve them, or you." She reached up and took his hand away from her face, but held onto it for a moment.

"Thank you, Grant. Thanks for being here." She dropped his hand and reached for the door handle, only to come up short when her seat belt locked her into place.

He chuckled and reached over to unbuckle it, but she'd turned at the same time. Their faces were inches apart, and all he could do was look into her dark eyes, transfixed by the richness he saw there. Before he knew what he was doing, his mouth was on hers in a soft kiss. Her hands went to his hair, neither pulling him away nor holding him in place. Instead, her fingers laced through his curls as if taking stock of each one.

Her mouth moved slowly under his and before

he knew it, their tongues touched and he melted into her sweet taste. She moaned, and then he moaned. Her fingers trailed down his neck, leaving a hot trail, but when he felt the ring on her finger scrape just under his ear, he pulled back and blinked.

"I'm sorry," he mumbled, realizing that she was still officially engaged to someone else.

She smiled. "You keep saying that." She reached up to pull him closer again, but he pulled back and shook his head. "I'm sorry." He knew he was repeating himself, but he didn't care. He knew she needed time to recover from the shock of losing Travis. He didn't want to be her rebound guy.

"It's just a kiss. It's not like I'm asking you to come up to my room." She smiled and he felt his face heat. How many times in the past years had he imagined just that? Even now, his mind was leading him up those stairs, stripping away her tight clothes, touching her soft…he shook his head clear.

"I better be going." He leaned back to his side of the truck, efficiently blocking the chance of them touching any more.

"Grant?" She waited until he looked over at her again. "Thanks for telling me the truth and for the ride home." She unbuckled her seat belt and got out of the truck. He watched her disappear into the dark house and wanted to kick himself.

The entire drive home, he berated himself for taking advantage of her. After all, she'd just found out that the man she'd been dating for almost eight years and was engaged to was cheating on her. Great, just great. Tell the girl of your dreams that the man of her dreams is a no-good, lying sack of shit, then kiss her until you can't see straight.

He drove the five miles to his new farm. When he turned off the highway into the long winding drive, he stopped at the top of the hill and looked down at his little valley. It was too dark to see now, but his mind played over every detail.

His stone house sat off to the left, a larger gray barn to the right. It held his three horses, five goats, two pigs, and two cattle. Off to the back, there was a small chicken coop between the barn and the house. It was all his. Every last spot of this place screamed his future. The future he'd decided he'd wanted three years ago after the tragic accident that had changed the course of his life forever. The second biggest secret he'd ever kept from uttering out loud.

Alex was in a deep slumber when she was attacked by a large, hairy creature. Its razor sharp fangs clawed out and scratched her on her arms, causing her to sit up and push the creature off her.

She felt bad when the small three-legged dog went flying off her mattress and landed with a small thump on the floor next to her bed.

"Oh, Buddy, I'm sorry." She reached for the small dog, only to have him scamper away. She jumped from the bed and raced after the little thing. He was surprisingly fast for a three-legged dog, but she finally caught up with him in the kitchen. She was down on her hands and knees and had just caught him and was giving him a hug and nuzzling her face into his soft fur, when she heard someone clear his throat.

Looking up through her mass of messy flyaway hair, she gasped. Grant sat with Chase at the kitchen table. Chase had a smile on his face, but Grant looked like he would have preferred to be anywhere but sitting at her kitchen table. His face was beet red, which only caused his blue eyes to look even bluer.

Dropping the small dog back on his three legs, she quickly stood up and watched Grant's eyes travel over her. Looking down at herself, she smiled a little when she realized that her white silk tank top and her shorts were almost completely see-through. She'd bought them at Victoria's Secret last month, and had hoped that they would be a wedding surprise for Travis, but after what had happened a few nights ago, she'd started wearing everything she'd bought for that lying, cheating….Shaking her head, she cleared her mind of Travis. Then she realized that this was the first time in two days that she'd been out of her bed and that she must look horrible. Quickly turning, she rushed from the room without saying a word.

Heading to the bathroom, she jumped in the shower and tried not to think about the last time she'd seen Grant. How could she have let herself get so carried away with the kiss? It had rocked her so much that it had been on her mind constantly for the few days.

After showering, she'd come up with the idea of clearing her mind by going on a long horseback ride after grabbing some food. She dressed quickly in her riding clothes and was a little sad when she walked back into the kitchen and saw that Grant was no longer present. Chase and Lauren sat at the table, eating sandwiches.

"Morning," she said as she walked over to the coffee pot and poured herself a large cup.

"Good afternoon," Lauren said and looked over her cup at her sister.

"Yes, well. I suppose it is. What was Grant Holton doing here?" She leaned back on the countertop and took a deep sip of the lukewarm coffee.

Chase actually giggled, then answered, "Getting an eyeful."

Lauren giggled, then she coughed and went back to reading the newspaper.

"Real funny." Alex smiled a little at her brother-in-law.

"You really ought to invest in a robe," Chase said, leaning back in his chair.

"I have several." Alex's chin went up and her smile grew even more. "But when that three-legged beast of yours goes on the prowl and attacks a sleeping person, you don't expect me to stop and put on a robe as I'm chasing the beast through the house, do you?"

Chase looked down at his feet at the sleeping dog in question. "Beast?" His eyebrows shot up. "You hear that, Buddy? You've never been called a beast before." Chase's smile got even bigger. "He's been called many things..." He ticked them off with his fingers as he named them. "Tripod, stumpy, gimpy, and my favorite, footloose, but never beast."

Alex laughed. "Okay, so the little guy woke me from a dead sleep, and I accidentally launched him off my bed." She walked over and picked the sleeping dog up. His eyes opened and his tail started wagging as he placed sloppy kisses all over her face. "I was just trying to apologize to the little guy, and didn't know you had company. I suppose I'll have to head over to his place and apologize."

"Oh, please," Haley said as she walked into the room. No doubt she'd been standing in the doorway behind Alex the entire conversation. Alex looked over at her younger sister; she looked like she'd been out working in the barn. Her clothes were covered with straw and sweat. "We all know that the last thing Grant wants from you is an apology." She chuckled as she walked to the refrigerator and pulled out a bottled water, taking a long drink before shutting the door. "Besides, he's still out back, loading up the hay he bought from Chase."

"He bought hay from us?" Alex walked to the kitchen window, but the barn was blocking any view other than the front of his dark truck.

"Yeah. He bought the farm down the road a while ago, but he hasn't had a chance to plant any hay on his fields this season. We had extra and could use the money," Lauren said, looking down at the paper.

"I'm going for a ride," Alex said to the room, then turned and walked out without another word.

She rushed across the yard, but slowed down when she reached the side of the barn. She could hear him moving the large hay bales around, but couldn't see him over the flat trailer, which was half full of bales. Looking back towards the house, she saw three sets of eyes peeking out the kitchen window at her. Straightening her shoulders, she turned the corner and bumped solidly into a bare, sweaty chest full of muscles. She tried to take a step back, but tan arms came up and held onto her.

"Sorry." She felt herself falling backwards, then forward, then backwards again. Finally, she landed sideways on a bale of hay. The wind was knocked out of her lungs as a very sweaty and half-naked Grant landed on top of her.

Instantly, she could hear laughing coming from the house and felt her back teeth grind as she tried to shove the heavy male off her. He was soaking her shirt with sweat. Now she'd need another shower before she could go riding. Then she looked up and lost her breath again.

Grant's hat was pushed back on his head. His eyes were laughing down at her, and his smile was contagious. She forgot all about his sweaty body lying on hers and started laughing with him. She didn't even know why she was laughing. He pushed up off her and the laughter dropped away. The muscles in his arms bulged as he did a push-up to remove his body from hers. When her laughter stopped, he paused and looked down at her. "I'm sorry, are you okay?"

She nodded her head, because her mouth had gone totally dry. There was no way she would have been able to form a single vowel, let alone put together a whole word. How had he gone from pudgy, glasses-wearing, zit-faced boy to this? Did he even need glasses anymore?

"Where are your glasses?" she asked looking up into his blue eyes. Had she ever realized his eyes were so blue behind those thick lenses?

He smiled a little and held himself above her. "I had Lasik eye surgery a few years back."

"Oh." She felt stupid lying under him, but didn't

really want him to move at the moment. She was sad when he finally did. He reached down and helped her stand.

"I guess I was too busy to notice you standing there." He picked a few strands of hay out of her hair. "I didn't hurt you, did I?"

"No." She shook her head. "You've lost so much weight, you're featherlight." She immediately regretted her words and blushed a little. His eyebrows shot up, then a quick smile formed on his lips.

"Thanks, I think."

"I just mean that…you look good." She bit her tongue and swore not to speak to him again until she could say something more intelligent. What was she doing? She was good at flirting. This was not like her to babble on like an ignorant schoolgirl. She was usually the one causing men to blush, not the other way around.

Now his smile grew to a full smile, even his eyes sparkled. "You look mighty good yourself."

She looked up at his eyes, held her shoulders back a little, then reached up and fixed his hat, straightening it on his head. She was happy when she saw his face turn a little pink.

"There, now you're perfect." She smiled.

Jill Sanders

Chapter Three

Grant's hands were shaking, so he shoved them deep in his jeans. He realized too late that he had a thick pair of leather gloves on and ended up looking like a fool. Alex chuckled, such a cute little sound, but he wondered just when he'd lost the upper hand.

"I'm going riding later." She stepped closer to him and the image of her standing in the kitchen a while ago popped into his mind. She'd stood in front of the sunny window with nothing but a see-through piece of silk on. He hoped that image would never leave his head. His mind had been so foggy that he hadn't heard the rest of what she'd said. "Huh?" He cleared his throat and tried to take a step back.

She smiled and moved with him, then took one more step until she was just a breath away from him. "I asked if you would like to go on a ride with me."

An image of the two of them wrapped together flashed so quickly in front of his eyes, he knew he turned a few shades of red.

"Um, sure. I just have to finish loading up." He motioned towards the almost-full flatbed trailer. He just couldn't think when she was almost pressing herself up against him. So close, in fact, that he could smell the sweetness of her.

He turned to finish the task and was a little unnerved when she sat down on a large bale of hay to watch him. He tried to get the chore done quickly and finished in record time. Strapping the hay down, he walked over to the fence where he'd set his water bottle and took a deep drink. The woman was trying to kill him. When she was around, he just couldn't control himself. His heart rate skipped and spiked like he was a jackrabbit being chased. He forced himself to think about the tasks he still had to complete at the farm; it was all he could do to keep his mind off her and on his work.

When he grabbed his shirt from the fence and started to pull it over his head, he thought he heard a low groan from her. Turning, he raised his eyebrows and asked, "Are you alright?"

She sighed and smiled. "Just dandy. Are you ready?" She stood and waited for him to walk towards her.

"Sure. Do you have a horse I can borrow?" He followed her into the dark barn.

"Sure, you can ride Carl. He's fairly new, but has proven to be a gentle giant." She smiled and walked over to a stall where a large, light-colored quarter horse stood. He loved animals, especially horses, so he walked up and, after letting Carl smell his hands, started stroking his mane.

"Carl, huh?" He smiled.

"Sure. I get to name some of the animals. I always hated giving them animal names." She leaned in and after looking around, whispered, "I like them to be human names, like Tanner or Sandy." Then she stood back. "After all, some of them are so human-like." She tilted her head and started rubbing Carl between his eyes. The horse closed its eyes and lowered its head, seemingly enjoying the pet. "Carl loves his name." She stepped back and smiled. "The saddles are over here." She walked towards the back of the barn. "Take your pick." Then she walked over to a light tan saddle and picked it up, carrying it to another stall.

He took his time picking a saddle that would fit his frame. He'd been raised around horses and knew a good saddle when he saw one. He had a good saddle of his own and had planned on getting a few newer ones before next year.

It took him a few minutes to find the rest of the gear, but after fifteen minutes, he had Carl all saddled up and ready to go.

She'd pulled a darker horse out into the yard and was just finishing tying down the saddle when he and Carl walked out of the barn.

Leaving Carl standing next to the fence with his reins tied to a post, he walked over and took Alex by the hips and helped her mount her horse. Her waist was so tiny that his fingers almost spanned her completely. She weighed next to nothing and he wanted to get his hands on her again, but he walked over to his horse and mounted in a quick, smooth motion. The horse pranced around a little, then settled down after he talked to him smoothly.

Leaning forward, he patted its mane. "Well," he looked at Alex, "where to?"

She smiled and pulled down her hat a little, letting two braids fall on either of her shoulders. "I was thinking to the south fence and back. It's around an hour there and back."

"Sound good to me. Lead the way." He nodded and pushed his hat a little farther down on his head so he wouldn't lose it if she wanted to go fast.

Just as they were starting to leave the yard, Haley rushed out of the house.

"Alex!" They both stopped. "I made you a snack. I know you've been out here for a few hours working hard, Grant, so I made you some sandwiches and drinks." She handed a full saddlebag to Grant and helped him tie it on the back of his horse.

"Thanks." He smiled down at Haley. "I would've been starving before we got back."

"Thanks, Haley." Alex smiled at her sister. Grant thought he saw humor in Haley's eyes, but he didn't know her well enough to tell if it was that or something else.

They made their way slowly across the north field. Here the trees and rolling hills of the southern side died away, leaving vast open fields of tall hay. Occasionally, a large oak tree would pop up out of the ground, giving shelter for the cattle that stood or lay below the wide branches. He loved this part of Texas, although he favored the more-wooded areas. When he looked around the fields, he could just imagine how it used to be hundreds of years ago, when the buffalo roamed these parts, wild.

"Are you going to tell me why you really moved back here?" she asked after they'd made it past a gate.

"What do you mean?" He looked over at her.

She shrugged her shoulders. "I don't know. There's just something you're not telling."

He chuckled. "You think someone would have to be mad to move back to Fairplay?"

"No, not that." She smiled. "But from what I've heard, you had a pretty cushy life out east. Everyone in town is wondering why you dropped everything to come home. And don't tell me it's to help your dad out." Her eyes narrowed and her lips

47

puckered a little.

He turned and looked straight ahead. "He does need my help. Mom can't get him to slow down and his blood pressure is higher than she likes."

"Was it a girl?" she asked, tilting her head at him.

"Was what a girl?" He wished the subject would change quickly.

"That caused you to come running home."

He shook his head lightly, not wanting to say anything else. He knew he wasn't able to keep secrets and decided a different tactic might work best. "How about we race to the next fence there." He nodded towards the horizon.

"If I win, will you tell me?" Her smile spread, lighting up her eyes. He couldn't help but nod.

"Fine," she called over her shoulder after she'd had already bolted on her horse. He dug his heels into Carl's sides and sent the horse after hers.

It took him no time to catch up to her horse, but halfway to the fence Carl started losing speed. "Come on, boy, we can whoop those two. Show them you're younger and stronger," he encouraged his horse. By the time they were a few yards from the fence, they were neck and neck again. When Alex pulled up, her horse was just a neck in front of his. He knew she would hound him until he told her the story of why he'd come home. But that didn't mean he couldn't do it on his own terms.

Pulling the horse next to hers, he smiled over at her. "Shall we find some shade and eat some lunch?" She was winded, but nodded. Part of him thought that he could have pushed the horse a little more, but he'd held back instead. Maybe, subconsciously, he wanted her to know why he had chosen to come home.

They walked the horses along the fence line until they found a small tree with dark green leaves that would shield them from the heat of the summer sun.

He took his time laying out a small blanket that Haley had folded in the other side of the saddlebag. Then he started pulling out small containers of food and smiled. Haley had thought of everything. There were sandwiches, chips, slices of apples and a container of grapes, some cheese, and a couple bottles of water. It had been a long time since he'd sat under the shade of a tree with a girl and had a picnic.

"This is nice." She leaned on her elbows on the blanket and watched him organize the plates of food. "I haven't been on a picnic since my sisters and I stayed at the cabin for Lauren's twenty-third birthday." She sighed and removed her hat, then leaned her head back.

"Travis never took you on a picnic?" he asked.

She laughed. "Travis never took me anywhere, let alone a picnic." Her eyes opened slightly and she looked at him. "I broke it off, you know.

Well…" she sat up a little. "I suppose not face-to-face, but I left him a voice mail." She sat up all the way and took a chunk of cheese, nibbling on it.

"You didn't think something like that required you to do it in person?"

"Did he have the nerve to tell me he was cheating on me?" Her shoulders went rigid.

"Easy," he said. "I'm on your side, remember?" He smiled, trying to get her to relax.

She shook her head, then closed her eyes. "I don't want to talk about Travis anymore." Then she sat up and looked at him. "You promised me you'd tell me what made you come back to Fairplay." She took the plate of food he offered her and sat it down in front of her, giving him her full attention.

He sighed. "You aren't going to let this go, are you?" When she shook her head, he sighed again. Then, to stall, he picked up his sandwich and took a large bite of turkey on wheat. Haley had packed some packets of spicy mustard, and he'd heaped it on. The zesty taste flooded his mouth, and he realized just how hungry he was.

He'd always loved food. Over the last five years, he'd learned to have a better relationship with not only food, but his body. It had been the hardest thing in the world for him to drop what most people called his baby fat. He knew the real reason he'd always stayed on the heavy side. His mother. To be more exact, his mother's southern cooking. She added butter, grease, sugar, and everything else that was unhealthy to every meal. She also demanded that he finished his plate, every time.

When he'd first moved away, he'd maintained his diet with fast food, pizzas, and anything else he could get his hands on in the dorms. Being one of the youngest college students at Harvard had taken a toll on his health, not to mention his mental state. He'd been picked on, beat up, and, even once, locked out of the dorms during a snowstorm.

"You know how I used to be." He looked at her and watched as understanding crossed her face.

"You mean being a little overweight?"

He chuckled. "That's putting it politely, but yes. It took me the first few years at Harvard to fit in. Even then, I was always somewhat of a loner. The complete opposite of how I felt here. Sure, I knew kids always made fun of me, but for the most part, I still considered everyone around here my friends." He took another bite, then plopped a few grapes into his mouth and chewed. "It wasn't until I started working for the law firm in Boston that I started thinking about coming home. The hours were long, the commute was a bitch." He looked over at her and winced. "Sorry." She smiled and nodded, so he continued. "Then I met Sam. I'd stuffed myself with Italian food one night, and the guilt had forced my feet to carry me all the way into a gym. Sam was a trainer there, and he took one look at me and refused to let me leave until I promised I'd be back first thing in the morning with a pair of tennis shoes and sweats." He smiled. "When a two-hundred-pound body builder threatens to hunt you down, you tend to show up early. Over the next year, he taught me how to eat right, exercise, and get healthy. Then one day, I walked into the gym and he was working with Terry. Terry was his younger sister. One thing led to another and we started sort-of dating." He picked up the bottle of water and took a deep drink.

"Do you still love her?" she asked, finishing off her sandwich.

He shook his head. "I never loved Terry. She was more like a friend who I hung out with. Terry didn't see it that way." He frowned, looking down at his half-eaten sandwich, feeling the sinking feeling in his gut. "She was what you would call high maintenance. She always wanted me to text her, to update my online status with everything we were doing. She wanted us to pose for pictures so she could post them online. It drove me nuts." He rolled his eyes.

Alex chuckled, and he stopped to look at her. She shrugged her shoulders. "Everyone knows someone like that. I'm not one of those kind of people. I don't even have a Facebook account," she said.

He smiled. "I didn't, either, until she opened one for me and took it over. Well, a year into our quote-unquote relationship, we decided to drive down with Sam and his girlfriend to the beach. Up until then, my relationship with Terry had been going pretty smoothly, if you don't count the compulsive updating she did. I had dropped all of my weight and was working with Sam to help out with his youth project. He ran free clinics for overweight youth at the Y, and I started tagging along, talking to the kids. It was weird seeing how far I'd come along in the eyes of those kids." He shook his head and took another drink.

"That's wonderful." She smiled at him. "I bet you really helped them out."

He nodded. "On the trip…" He took a deep breath and closed his eyes. "We were halfway up the coast, heading to a little place outside of Portland. Sam was driving, and he swerved to avoid a deer. The car spun and went head on into a tree."

"Oh!" she gasped.

"Sam died on impact." His heart still hurt when he thought of it. "Terry and I and Sam's girlfriend, Julie, ended up with only minor scratches." His eyes stung when he thought back at it, seeing his Hercules-like friend that way. "Things changed after the accident. Terry changed. She became more obsessed. She always wanted to know where I was, who I was with. At first I put it off as her way of recovering from her brother's death, but then I logged onto my Facebook account, and she'd posted that we were engaged to be married." He shook his head. "So," he sighed, "I broke it off. I felt terrible, but I wasn't ready to commit to her."

He shook his head.

He didn't know why it mattered so much what Alex thought of him, but he was holding his breath until she spoke. Until she told him what she thought of him.

When she reached over and took his hand, he could see the sincere look in her eyes. "You did the right thing to break things off. I guess that makes two of us."

Chapter Four

"How did she take it?" Alex asked, after a moment of silence.

He shook his head and frowned. "Not good. She posted things online that eventually caused the firm I was working for to seriously question if they wanted to continue letting me work there."

"How horrible. That bitch." She watched as he smiled and his eyes softened.

"I think she was just misdirected. Losing her only brother like that loosened a few things in her head. At least I like to think that."

"And here I was, concerned about breaking it off with Travis." She shook her head and felt her stomach sink a little. "It's not that I don't want to hurt him after what he's put me through." She shook her head. "I'd like to string him up on the largest tree downtown by his toenails." Grant chuckled. "It's just that I know he always seems to talk his way back into a relationship with me. We've broken up ten times over the last three years," she blurted out. "I don't know how he does it. One minute we're broken up, the next we're back together." She frowned down at her hands. "I'm afraid I won't have the strength to stand against him. Especially now that it really matters."

His hand came up under her chin and pulled her face up until she was looking into his blue eyes. "Maybe you just haven't had the right reason to stay away." He leaned closer to her and her breath caught.

Then his mouth was on hers, and his fingers pulled her closer to him. He smelled like sweat and saddle leather, and the mixture was intoxicating to her. His skin sent little tingles everywhere he touched her. His tongue rubbed gently over her lips until she opened for him, playing the tip of her tongue over his, shyly. Then he tilted her head more and took the kiss deeper. She moaned and ran her hands up his jeans, playing her fingers over the muscles she found in his thighs. He pulled her closer until she was almost sitting on his lap. Trailing kisses down her neck, he pulled open the buttons on her checkered shirt. She wore a spaghetti strapped tank top underneath. He pushed her shirt off her shoulders and pulled back and looked at her. Just looked. She'd never been looked at like that before. Like she was something precious. Something to be treasured. It made her go warm inside until she wanted him to touch her, everywhere and quickly.

Then he was kissing her again, and they were falling backwards onto the blanket. Her shirtfront was opened, allowing him to run his hands over the light material of her undershirt as he kissed his way down her collarbone. He pushed her shirt up, slowly letting his fingers walk upward until he cupped her gently. Her head rolled back and she moaned with delight as his fingers pinched her nipples softly. She arched her back, trying to get closer, pushing her breast into his hands further. She felt him smile next to her skin and wrapped her fingers in his hair, pulling him where she wanted him to be. His hot mouth hovered over her sensitive bud as it puckered through the soft material. Finally, he dipped his mouth lower, using his tongue to wet the cotton and sending waves of pleasure pulsing through her entire body. She wrapped her legs around his hips, pulling him next to her as she felt his desire against her core.

She wanted him. She wanted him right now. In her fields, on the picnic blanket. She moved slowly, rubbing her core against his erection. He gasped then moaned and continued to lap at her nipples. When he pulled her shirt up, exposing her to the warmth of the day, she sighed. He looked down at her, his hand resting on her flat stomach as he smiled.

"Beautiful," he murmured just before dipping his head and setting his tongue to her bare skin.

She reached under his shirt, yanking and pulling until finally he sat up and tossed it aside, then quickly came back down to where he'd left. He ran his mouth over every inch of her exposed skin. Her hands traveled over his muscles, his shoulders, his pecs. Then she leaned up and tasted his heated skin. Salt and sin. She'd never experienced anything like it. He tasted like a man and felt absolutely wonderful pressing her down into the blanket.

When her hands reached for the buttons on his jeans, his hands came over hers and pulled them up and away. She must have made a noise, because he chuckled.

"There's plenty of time. No need to rush," he said against her belly button. "Let me just savor you." He released her hands to run his fingers over her hips, then he tugged lightly, lowering her jeans until the tops of her white laced panties were exposed. "Beautiful," he said again. "Your skin is so soft here." He ran a finger lightly over the dip in her hips. "And here." He crossed her stomach slowly, taking the time to dip his finger just below her belly button. "I want to touch you, every inch." She looked up into his eyes and saw the heat there that matched her own.

"Yes, please." She reached for his hands, only for him to grip her wrists again. Then he smiled down at her and shook his head.

"You go too fast." He laid her hands by her side, then slowly unzipped her jeans, pulling them lower until they were down by her knees and boots. He shook his head and chuckled. "Boots are always the problem. We'll leave them on for now." She wanted to object, but he'd dipped his head again and was running his mouth where his fingers had just been. Her hands went into his hair again, enjoying the soft curls she felt there. When his mouth dipped lower and hovered just above her panties, she thought she'd go crazy from wanting. Travis had never, could have never, brought her to such want before. Looking down at Grant's head, she smiled. Grant was not Travis, the only man she'd ever been with like this before. Grant wouldn't be the selfish lover Travis had always been, never bringing her to a point of enjoyment before he took his own.

Grant pulled her panties to the side and set his tongue on her sensitive skin, causing her shoulders to bolt up from the blanket, her hands fisted in his hair as he lapped at her, using his mouth and tongue to spread her sensitive skin. His hands gripped her hips, holding her still while he repeated the motion over and over until she closed her eyes and screamed with her release.

Alexis lay there, looking at the sky through the thick cover of leaves on the branches above her and realized that she'd had her very first orgasm. Why, oh, why hadn't she done this years ago? She knew the answer as soon as her mind had asked the question. Travis.

Then blue eyes came to hover over her and she

smiled as Grant looked down into her face. "Do you think that was distracting enough?"

She smiled even more and pulled him down towards her. "I'm not sure. Maybe you better finish the job."

He chuckled. "Next time. I think it's about time I got back. I've got to unload all this hay tonight." He helped her pull her pants back into place, but before he allowed her to pull her shirt back down, he ran his fingers over her soft skin one last time. "Beautiful." He smiled at her.

She watched him put his shirt back on and thought the same thing about him. Next time, she thought. She was going to make sure there was a next time, and that meant dealing with Travis once and for all.

When they rode up the barn a little under an hour later, she was so relaxed she almost didn't see the blue truck parked in front of her car. When she noticed Travis sitting behind the wheel, her shoulders straightened and she felt a sharp pain in the left side of her temple. She knew she needed to deal with him, but she'd hoped to do it later that week.

"What me to stick around?" Grant whispered as he helped her off the horse. She shook her head, and he nodded his head at Travis as he approached.

"Hey there, Grant." Travis walked over and planted a kiss on her mouth. She hadn't had any time to dodge it, and when she'd turned her head, he'd still gotten half of her lips. He tasted like cigarettes and beer. She pushed him away and handed the horse reins to Grant, who walked the horses into the barn.

"I don't like that guy sniffin' after you. What's he doing here anyway?" Travis pulled her a few steps away, towards the back of Grant's truck.

"Loading up hay." She nodded towards the truck.

"Well, men who work for you shouldn't have their hands all over you. It's not right. You're my fiancée after all."

She took a step away from him. "No, I'm not. Not anymore. Especially not after what you and Savannah did in your truck on my birthday."

She watched his eyes open wide, like he was shocked. The thought of Travis and Savannah making out turned her stomach. How long had it been going on?

"Listen…" He took her arm and pulled her to the back of the barn where no one would see or hear them. "I was drunk, you know that. After you walked away, Savannah came up and started attacking me. I didn't mean to sleep with her."

She gasped. "You actually slept with her?" Her voice had risen to a high pitch. "You slept with her on my birthday?" She reached down and removed the ring from her finger and tossed it at his chest. "Goodbye, Travis. I don't want to talk to you or see you on my property again. If I do, I'll shoot your

61

sorry ass." She turned and walked into the house, shaking the entire way up to her room, where she slammed the door and sat quietly on her bed. For the first couple minutes, her mind was blank as she listened to Travis' truck drive away. Then she released the breath she'd been holding and felt free. For the first time in years, she felt free. She'd never thought of their relationship as a burden before, but somehow, spending the last few hours with Grant had forced her to open her eyes to the possibilities that were out there. Not just physically. Knowing what Grant had gone through in Boston really helped her put things into perspective.

She didn't need Travis. She didn't need any man. Sure, she enjoyed having one on her arm, but the thought of getting into another relationship like she'd had with Travis didn't seem appealing to her. She was going to live her life, do what she wanted for once.

Looking around the room, she realized she didn't know exactly what that was. She'd been dating Travis since a week after her seventeenth birthday. He was the only man she'd let touch her, until today. Her mind turned and an image of Grant's head as he pleased her appeared in her mind. She blushed, her cheeks heating, and she felt herself melt and get wet thinking about what he'd done. Travis had never done anything like that. Oh, she'd known it was possible, since her friends had talked openly about their relationships, but she'd never had it done to her before.

Thinking about it, she realized there was a lot she hadn't experienced before. Maybe Grant was the right man to show her everything that she'd been missing? After all, there was no fear of her falling in love with him, since she'd always think of him as the good guy, and everyone in town knew that there was no way she would ever fall for anyone that pure.

Grant cussed in the empty barn for the tenth time. Sweat dripped down every inch of his body and every muscle in his body ached. His jeans were completely covered in sweat, dust, and hay. He looked down at the animals watching him from the main floor in his barn and laughed. They actually looked concerned for him.

"Don't worry, guys, I'll have this unloaded today." He got back to hauling the bundles up the ladder stairs and wondered why he hadn't hired someone to help him unload it all. Not only had he spent the last two days doing his normal chores around the large place, but he'd spent as much time as he could hauling the hay up a dozen rickety stairs to his loft.

The last two days had been hell not only on his body; his mind refused to stop focusing on the picnic with Alex. He couldn't stop thinking about her sweet taste on his tongue. It had taken all his willpower to stop that day, under the tree.

He knew she was just getting over a hard breakup and didn't want her to use him. Like he'd used her. Hell. He cussed at himself. He'd done what he'd done for a purpose. So she would know how good it could be. To show her what it could be like. He'd wanted to take her then and there, but something inside had stopped him. She wasn't ready. He knew it.

In the end, it took him a hundred times longer to unload the truck then it had to load it, because he kept stopping and thinking about her. By the time he walked into his house on the third night, all he could think about was a shower and his bed. When he walked inside, he saw the little red light flashing on his answering machine, which made him realize he hadn't stopped in town to purchase a new cell phone. Since he was enjoying hiding from the world, he didn't mind just having the home line and an old-fashioned answering machine.

Hitting the button, he listened to his mother remind him about some out-of-state dinner guest and say that he shouldn't forget to wear his nice new tie she'd bought him. It wasn't until halfway through his shower that he remembered that the dinner his mother had been talking about was tonight. He groaned and looked at the clock on the bathroom wall. He was due to be at his folks' house in less than an hour. He groaned again.

Pulling his tired muscles out of the shower, he put on his best clothes and the tie his mother wanted him to wear. He wished his younger sister, Melissa, was in town instead of attending school in Dallas. Then maybe his mother wouldn't be trying to feed him all the time.

On his last visit, he had finally convinced his father that he was man enough to fill his own plate, instead of letting his mother pile her fried chicken and mashed potatoes a mile high. His mother hadn't been so pleased. She kept trying to sneak more food onto his plate, claiming he was getting too thin.

When he drove up to the simple one-story house, he spotted two cars he didn't recognize. Just what he wanted, a dinner with a bunch of strangers. When he walked into the house, he could hear his mother's laughter from the den and walked in to the back room. There was an older couple sitting on the couch. He walked over and kissed his mother on the cheek, waiting to be introduced.

His mother jumped up from her chair and patted his arm. "Oh! There he is now. Roger, Regina, this is our son, Grant." His mother's fingers dug into his back, forcing him to step forward and shake their hands. He must have mumbled something like, "How do you do?" to them, because they both nodded and replied. Then his father stepped in the back door, his grilling apron wrapped around his larger belly. "Oh, there you are my boy. I was just telling Terry that you'd be along shortly."

Grant's heart started beating faster. He felt every vein in his body as it sped up and started beating frantically. When his ex-girlfriend walked into his parents' house holding a glass of wine in one hand, his head almost exploded. She had a large smile pasted on her face and a worried look in her eyes.

"Would you excuse me for a moment?" he said between his teeth, then he grabbed her arm and walked outside with her. When they were alone, he turned to her. "What in the hell are you doing here?"

"What?" She looked shocked at him. "Didn't you get my messages? My parents were visiting from California and wanted to meet you." She looked down at her hands. "For Sam's sake." She crossed her arms over her chest, then glared up at him.

"Those are your parents?" He turned and looked towards the house. Just great, he thought. "What have you told them about us?" He turned back towards her, pinning her with a stare.

She tried to avoid his answer by walking past him, but he grabbed her arm again. He hadn't seen her in almost a year. Other than the fact that her hair was shorter, nothing else had changed, and it appeared the way she thought about him hadn't either. "Terry. What?"

"They may still think that we're engaged, since I never really updated our Facebook page." She sighed and looked away.

"I'm not doing this." He turned and walked into his parents' house, Terry close on his heels. "Mr. and Mrs. Walkins." He waited until they both looked at him. "I want you to know that Terry and I were never really engaged and that we broke up over a year ago." He felt Terry's fingernails dig into his arm. "I'm sorry about Sam. He was one of my best friends for over five years. There isn't a day that goes by that I don't remember his advice and training. Even up against one of the best cooks in the south." He nodded towards his mother, who beamed back at him, her hands going over her heart. "I'm sorry you came all this way to meet me under the assumption that we were engaged. I hope you weren't deceived." He waited.

"Thank you." Terry's mother, Regina, stood and smiled at him. "We assumed your relationship had been broken off once we heard you had moved back home and Terry was still staying in Boston." Her husband stood next to her. "I hope this won't hinder the wonderful dinner your parents have planned for us. Your father has been grilling the most delicious smelling steaks and your mother promised me a copy of her peach cobbler recipe."

He smiled quickly. "Not at all." Then he held his hand out again and shook Roger's hand once more. "It truly is an honor to meet you both."

Three hours later he drove back up his driveway, thinking about how Sam and Terry had come to be some of the best friends he'd had in

Boston. Terry still had her quirks, but by the time his mother had served up dessert, he believed Terry was no longer under the assumption that they were an item.

They'd talked about the online business Grant's father was trying to start with him. He was on board even knowing he was most likely going to be doing all the work. It was a legal advice site that would help customers with basic legal filings and paperwork. They'd found a company in Houston to design the site and they had done all the background work for them. All they had left were some small basic things, which his father was currently taking care of. His dad had talked in great detail about the business with Regina and Roger. They'd been so interested that his father had pulled out his laptop and they'd spent almost an hour going over everything. Now Grant's eyes burned, as well as every muscle in his body.

When he hit his bed after taking his boots and tie off, he fell face-first into his soft mattress and was out like a light.

Chapter Five

$\mathcal{A}$lex had been working at Mama's Diner since her sophomore year. She loved working for Jamella, aka Mama, the owner. Jamella was in her late sixties and was big enough that most everyone gave her space and respect. Mama's Diner had been hers for the past twenty years. Jamella knew everyone's business and everything there was to know about the small town of Fairplay.

Mama had been like a surrogate mother to Alex ever since her own mother had died in that tornado when she was just six. Since then, Jamella had treated the three sisters like they were her own, and they loved her for it.

Not only did Alex love the job, she loved the people. Seeing almost everyone in the small town had its perks. You were always up-to-date on the gossip and the first to hear any news. She even enjoyed working there when it meant serving the woman who had broken up her engagement.

It was a few days after her picnic with Grant that she "accidentally" spilled a whole plate of spaghetti over Savannah Douglas' white lace dress. She had apologized profusely while using the greasiest rag in the kitchen to help her wipe the mess off her new dress. Once Savannah had screamed loud enough that everyone in the next two counties could hear her, she marched out of the restaurant, threatening to sue Mama.

When Alex went back into the kitchen, Jamella and Willard, the longtime cook, were laughing so hard, Alex had to join in.

"You sure showed dat girl. Maybe now she keep her oily hands to herself," Jamella said in her Louisiana drawl. She smiled and slapped Willard's shoulder.

"It did feel good." Alex crossed her arms over her chest and leaned against the countertop, smiling. But her good mood went away later that evening when she overheard one of the clerks from the Grocery Stop talking to Patty Nolan, Travis' mother, who was a regular at Mama's, about how the Holton's had had out-of-town visitors earlier. Alex had been dealing with Patty ever since she'd started dating Travis. The woman always seemed to have her nose in their business, but after a while, Alex had found a method for dealing with her. She pretty much ignored her.

From what she'd overheard, it seemed that Grant's fiancée and her parents had come into town for dinner. Alex's heart dropped.

Grant was engaged? She kept trying to persuade herself that it didn't matter. After all, she'd been pretty much using him, right? And she had planned to keep using him to help her get over Travis and the whole ordeal. Then she got angry. How dare he use her like that! She tried to shake the thought out of her mind, but for the rest of her shift, the whole mess kept playing over and over in her head. By the time she left the dark parking lot, she had a slight throbbing behind her eyes. She didn't know what sent her driving past the turn off to Saddleback Ranch, but she found herself heading towards Grant's farm. When she pulled up and saw that his bedroom light was still on, she slammed the car door and marched to the front porch. She knocked until someone answered, praying the whole time that it wasn't some half-dressed woman.

Instead, she was greeted by a very angry Grant, who was shoeless and looked like he'd slept in his clothes.

"What?" He drew up and shut his mouth quickly when he saw who was banging on his door at one in the morning. "Alex? What are you doing here?" He looked around. "Are you in some sort of trouble?"

"What? No." She looked past him, trying to see if there was anyone inside with him. Maybe they had just started undressing each other?

"Then I'll repeat my first question. What are you doing here?"

"I…" Her mind went blank. She'd driven here and banged on his door, expecting to find his arms wrapped around some other woman, but she had never expected to have to explain herself. "I heard you had dinner with your fiancée's family," she blurted out.

He looked at her, and his eyebrows slowly went up in question.

She sighed and crossed her arms over her chest. "Grant Holton, are you going to let me in or are you going to make me stand out here trying to see if you're alone in that house."

His smile was quick. "Alexis West, would you please come in." He bent at the waist and bowed, waiting for her to walk past him. Then he turned and shut the door with his foot. "As you can see, it's just me. You're welcome to come and check under my bed, if you feel so inclined." She turned and saw him flash a smile at her.

"That won't be necessary." She walked into a large room, which she happily noticed was his living room. Walking over, she sat on the couch and started biting her nails. She never bit her nails unless she was nervous. How was she going to explain herself to him?

He walked over and sat across from her, then rubbed his hands over his face.

"I'm sorry if I woke you. I worked the late shift at Mama's and overheard Jenny, the clerk at the Grocery Stop, talking about your mother coming in, bragging about cooking dinner for some out-of-town guests..."

She stopped when he groaned. She looked up at him, in question.

"Now it'll be all over town." He put his head in his hands and shook it. "Just great."

"Will you please tell me what is going on?" She sat forward.

"It was Terry. She dragged her parents all the way from California to meet me. Well, they'd wanted to meet me anyway, for Sam's sake, but she neglected to mention that we'd broken it off over a year ago, oh, and that we were never really engaged."

She released the breath she'd been holding and leaned back in the couch. "Is that all?" When he nodded, she started laughing so hard she had to hold her sides.

"You think this is funny?" He looked at her like she was crazy.

"Yes." She nodded her head. "I spilled hot spaghetti sauce all over Savannah's new white dress today, then proceeded to mop it up with the oiliest rag I could find, and you spent a night having dinner with a crazy ex-girlfriend and her parents." She laughed some more.

Then she looked at him and noticed he was frowning.

"What?" She dropped her smile a little. "What's wrong?"

"You're still crazy for Travis, aren't you?"

"Of course I am." She smiled a little. "Crazy *is* the right word. I've come to realize that I stopped loving him years ago." She leaned back again and looked at him. "I think I was in love with being in love. I had always wanted what my folks had." She sighed and looked off, past his shoulder. "I remember them dancing in the kitchen, holding each other. I never heard my pa say a bad word about my ma, nor the other way around. I suppose I was hoping one day that Travis and I would be like that."

When she looked at him again, he was smiling. "Why Alexis West, you're a romantic."

She balked. "No I'm not. You take that back."

Then he was laughing. "That's a good thing, sweetheart."

She started blushing. "Oh." She shook her head. "I must be tired." She looked down and fiddled with the bottom of her uniform skirt.

"Where you really upset over the possibility of me being engaged?" He walked over and sat next to her.

"No." She pulled her hand out of his.

"Alex?" He put his fingers under her chin and turned her head towards his.

"Fine, yes. I was trying to figure out what I could spill on you the next time you walked through Mama's doors." She pulled back and crossed her arms.

He leaned forward and kissed her quickly. "Thanks."

"What for?" She wanted him to kiss her again.

"In a roundabout way, you just told me that you care about me." He smiled and she noticed for the first time that he had a slightly crooked smile. Had he always had that? And why hadn't she noticed how sexy his smile and his eyes were before? Before she could say anything, however, a large yawn escaped her.

"I'm sorry. I pulled a double shift today. I've missed a couple days work this last week." She yawned again. He smiled at her.

"Don't worry about it. I was so tired during dinner the other day that my mom had to keep kicking me under the table when I would nod off." He chuckled. "If you want, you're welcome to crash in my spare bedroom upstairs."

She stretched her arms over her head and thought of how wonderful it would be to sleep in a room next to him, in his house, or next to him in his bed. Then shook her head. "That's okay. I want a shower and my own bed. Thank you, though." She stood up and smiled when he quickly followed, then pulled her close for another kiss.

"Alex?"

"Hmmm?" she said against his lips.

"How is it that you can make grease and coffee smell so sexy?" He nibbled on her neck for a moment. She chuckled and pulled back.

"I'm sorry for barging in on you this late. I suppose I wasn't thinking clearly." She pushed her hair back out of her eyes. No doubt she looked like the tangled mess she felt like.

"Any time." He smiled and walked her to the door.

When she got home, she tiptoed past her sisters' bedrooms. She doubted she would even make it through a shower, so instead, she filled the new garden tub that Chase had installed a few months back. Resting her head against the pillow while the hot water soothed her muscles, she dreamed of Grant.

Grant was beginning to wonder if he had gone crazy. He was a lawyer, not a farmer. His animals meant a lot to him, and he was driven to take good care of them, but sometimes he just wished they could talk.

He'd called Chase over more times than he wanted to admit, afraid that one animal or another was sick. Chase had assured him that every one was perfectly healthy.

But now he stood looking down at one of his goats, Mojo, wondering why she wouldn't get up. He'd sat with her for the last few minutes before rushing into the house and frantically calling Chase, who had arrived just in time to see the first kid being born.

"Why didn't you tell me she was pregnant?" Grant asked. He looked over at Chase, who just laughed.

"I never got a look at her before. You had me look at all the other animals first. Besides, you should have been able to tell by looking at her."

"I thought she was just fat," Grant said, sitting next to her on the hay floor, holding her head. He looked up in time to see Chase shaking his head and laughing.

"Here comes another one." Less than ten minutes later the third and final girl was born.

"Congratulations." Chase slapped Grant's back and laughed, watching the first two kids stumble around the small space. "You're the proud papa of triplets."

He kept his friend there for over an hour asking him question after question. What did they eat?

What shots did they need? And more important, what did the mama need?

Chase was patient and answered all his questions, even showing him how to clean the little girls up, but Mojo was doing a fine job of it herself. Then they reloaded the small stall with fresh hay and Grant walked Chase back to his truck.

"Heard your folks had some company the other night." Chase leaned against his truck and smiled.

Grant groaned. "Yeah. What's the best way to spread a rumor around town that I'm not engaged?"

Chase laughed. "You could start dating every available girl in the county." Then he chuckled. "Or tell everyone you're secretly married. That seemed to work well for me." They laughed.

Later that night, Grant swung out to the barn to check up on the new family. The kids were snuggled down fast asleep in a corner. Mojo, on the other hand, looked wired. He sat and talked to her for a while, then made his normal night rounds. During his nightly routine, he'd come up with a plan to get the rumors stopped around town.

The next day, he walked into Mama's Diner with the biggest bouquet of flowers he could buy at the Grocery Stop, making sure to write the little note within sight of the clerk and a few of the ladies standing in line behind him. He sat down at the booth and waited for Alex to walk out from the back room. Then he stood and, to the surprise of her and everyone else in the diner, swept her into a long, heated kiss, then handed her the flowers.

"Oh, Grant," she beamed, "these are beautiful." He could see a hint of humor in her eyes and wondered if she knew what he was doing.

"I saw them and thought of you and of our picnic the other day." He actually heard several people start to gossip right there in the diner and felt like laughing.

"They're perfect." Then she stepped closer and hung her free arm around his neck and purred. "How about another picnic this weekend?" She smiled and winked at him. He could only nod in reply and was sure his face had just turned a deep shade of red in front of half the town of Fairplay.

By the time he'd driven home after a very long lunch and dessert at the diner, he was sure the gossip had changed about him around town. If his name was going to be tied to anyone, he wanted to make sure it was someone he was actually actively pursuing.

He parked his truck in front of the barn and decided to check on the animals. He didn't know what made him choose to go inside the barn instead of the house, but something called him to step into the building.

When he opened the door, the smell of gasoline hit him immediately. Throwing the door wide, he started to frantically look around. He didn't smell fire, but knew that there was no way he'd left that much gas in the barn.

Less than five minutes later, he was rushing into the house to call the sheriff. He'd left everything where he'd found it. By the time Stephen Miller, the local sheriff who'd been in office since Grant was two feet high, pulled in to park behind his truck, he was steaming.

"Now, Grant. What do you mean someone tried to burn down your barn. It's still standing." The older man slammed his car door and took off his hat to wipe his sweaty brow.

"Someone wanted to burn it down, Sheriff." He'd spent the time waiting for the sheriff getting all of his animals out of the fume-filled building. "Just have yourself a look." He motioned towards the door.

"Whoo-wee." The sheriff stood back and waved his hat in front of his face. "What do you have in there?" He walked in and looked around. Grant knew what he'd find. Someone had poured four of his five-gallon buckets of tractor fuel all over the barn. They had even splattered some on the animals. But what had really disturbed him was the matchbook sitting right inside the barn doors. It had been a warning.

"They wanted me to know they could have burned it all down." He stood just behind the sheriff, who was looking down at the matchbook from Mama's Diner.

"Well, damn." The sheriff banged his hat against his leg. "I guess we'll need to sit down and find out who you've pissed off lately."

Grant laughed sharply. There was only one name running through his mind. It was the first one that had popped into his head when he'd seen the matchbook.

"Travis Nolan."

The sheriff turned towards him quickly. "Now Grant, don't you go throwing that name out too quickly. We both know any trouble that boy gets into, his pa is going to sweep it under the rug so fast, I can't even finish filling out my paperwork."

"I know it was him. I stopped by the diner today and publicly made a move on Alexis." Grant registered the smile on the sheriff's face. Then the old man whistled.

"Didn't even let the dust settle before you started to make a play on that girl, did you?" He smiled again.

"No sir, not when I've waited forever for her." He smiled a little when the sheriff patted him on the back.

"You're a good kid, you know that. You take after your folks." Then he turned and looked back into the empty barn. "Well, I guess I'll fill out this paperwork and see how far we get. I'll swing by the Nolan's and ask Travis' whereabouts. When did you say you left the house?" He pulled out a little notepad and asked Grant a few questions before walking through the barn looking for anything else out of place.

It took the rest of the evening for Grant to get the gas-soaked hay out of the barn. The son of a bitch hadn't, thankfully, crawled up the ladder and gotten any gas on the stacked hay. But it still ate at him while he shoveled and used the wheelbarrow to pull load after load of ruined hay out of the barn. Once the place was fairly gasoline-free, he moved the animals back in and fed and watered them. Then he drove into town and bought himself a couple heavy-duty locks for both the front door and the back door of the barn. He even grabbed a smaller one for his chicken coop.

Just around sunset, he watched Alex's car drive up and park behind his truck. When she got out, he smiled at the pretty sundress she was wearing. The turquoise blue suited her.

"Evening." He'd showered off the stench of gas and was sitting out on the porch trying to muster up enough strength to cook some chicken on the grill. "You look mighty pretty tonight. Would you like to stay for dinner?" He walked over to her and pulled her close as she smiled and wrapped her arms around his neck.

"I hear you had some trouble out here." She frowned. "Listen, Grant, I didn't mean to cause…"

"Hush now, you had nothing to do with it and you know it. If you go around making excuses for that sorry sack of…" He shook his head. "No harm was done. Just some soiled hay. He was just being a sore loser. What about staying for dinner?"

She smiled and nodded. "I heard you have some new goats." He smiled and took her hand and started walking her towards the barn.

"First we'll see the goats, then we'll go out back and grill us some chicken." He stopped and pulled her into his arms. "Then I'll take you inside and have you in my bed." He smiled down at her and was pleased when he saw a light flush on her cheeks. He'd never caused her to blush before. It had always been the other way around. He realized he could get used to having the upper hand.

Chapter Six

$\mathcal{A}$lex's breath hitched. She'd been nervous the short drive over to his place. She knew why she'd taken her time, putting on her prettiest dress, an extra spritz of perfume, and even her brand new pair of underwear. She was going to sleep with Grant Holton, and she was going to enjoy every second of her time.

When she turned down his drive, she stopped and tried to level her breathing since she'd never been this nervous with anyone before. She looked at his house. The place had belonged to several other people in the past, and it was their nearest neighbor. It was a Verde-style stone ranch with a red tiled roof. It looked like it belonged in the hills of California instead of East Texas. He'd changed a few things around the place. He'd added a large wood swing on the front porch and had painted the barn a bright red. There were some new bushes and flowers out front and along the drive.

It had taken all her willpower not to turn back around and just drive home. It had nothing to do with Travis, and everything to do with how nervous she felt about the new experience she was about to have. She knew this was a necessary step in getting over things and moving on. Finally, she drove up. He was standing on the front porch, looking sexy in jeans and a gray shirt. He smiled and everything felt right.

He took her hand, breaking her out of the spell, and walked her towards the barn. There was a faint smell of gasoline lingering in the air. She'd found out what had happened when the sheriff had come into Mama's to question her and Jamella. He'd asked if they had seen Travis hanging around and if she knew if Travis had a matchbook from Mama's.

Jamella had laughed at that one. Everyone in town had a matchbook from the diner. They sat in a huge bowl right by the cash register. Jamella had ordered a thousand of them a few years back from a company in China, but the order had been messed up and she'd gotten ten thousand instead. They couldn't give the darn things away fast enough. There were still ten boxes of them sitting in the attic at the diner.

Alex blinked a few times to let her eyes adjust to the dim barn. Then they walked over to a short, small stall where three new goats were running around, butting each other and playing.

"Their mother is in the other stall. She's pretty much tired of them and needed a break." He laughed as the three goats noticed them. All were now standing with their front feet on the bottom rung of the gate, their short tails moving fast as they begged for attention.

"Oh, aren't you three so cute." Alex leaned over and tried to pet all of them, each one pushing the others out of the way. "What have you named them?" She looked up at Grant.

He shook his head. "Hadn't thought about it yet. They're all females." Then he smiled. "You always had a way with naming animals. What do you think?"

"Well…" She stood up and thought about it. "Names for three sisters…" She tapped her chin and paced a few steps away, then turned and walked back. "There were the three sisters in the Greek mythology of the Gorgons, but those were evil and ugly sisters." She looked down at the cute goats. Then a big smile crossed her face. "I've got it! Three sisters, too. How about the Powerpuffs?"

His eyebrows shot up, then he laughed. "Blossom, Bubbles, and Buttercup?"

When she nodded, he continued. "That's just rich." He laughed again and nodded to the next stall where a black-headed goat was demanding attention. "Mojo there is their mother."

She looked at him, then giggled. "Don't tell me you named her Mojo Jojo."

87

He smiled. "I didn't, but the daughter of the farmer I bought her had, and well, the name stuck."

"Then it's settled." She turned back to the goats. "Now we just need to decide who is who?"

He laughed, then tugged on her hand and pulled her into his arms. "I have a few pigs out back that I haven't named yet." He smiled down at her and she felt her heart skip. When his head dipped, she enjoyed the feel and taste of his lips against hers. His taste was intoxicating, and she was very thankful that he didn't smoke. Travis had always tasted of cigarettes.

Grant pulled back and brushed her hair aside. "If we keep doing that, we'll wind up skipping dinner all together."

"I don't mind." She tried to pull him back down, but heard his stomach growl loudly and smiled. "But I guess you do."

He laughed. "I've been working hard all day."

She sat out on his brick patio and watched as he barbecued chicken with some corn and potatoes over the open grill. She realized she'd never grilled out with Travis either. Come to think of it, there was a lot she hadn't done with Travis. He'd never taken her out for an official date. Sure, they'd eaten at Mama's or at his parents' place several times. They had even driven through a drive-thru in Tyler on multiple occasions, but he'd never dressed up and taken her out for a fancy dinner before. They'd never gone to the movies together, never—

"What are you frowning about? I promise you my cooking isn't that bad." Grant came and sat across from her.

"I'm sorry." She shook her head clear of Travis and his many faults, then smiled at Grant. "It's so hard, thinking of all the things I've missed." She took a deep breath and leaned back in her chair and looked around.

He tilted his head. "Yeah? Like what?" He took a drink of his tea and watched her.

"Like dates. Real dates." She got up and walked to the edge of the grass. "Hay rides in the fall, making out in a movie theater. Stuff like that. Travis never wanted to do anything with me, not anything in public, anyway." She blushed, realizing what she'd just admitted to. "Sure, he liked to go to the Rusty Rail and hang out with his friends." She turned and frowned. "I always imagined I'd have a long line of guys waiting to take me out." She sighed and looked off into the distance." She chuckled, then turned again. He sat there, looking at her with a slight smile on his face and she felt like a fool. She hadn't meant to tell him all that.

He stood up and walked towards her. "I always imagined you'd have a long line of guys beating each other up just to win your hand." He picked up her hand and brushed his lips across her knuckles. It was the most romantic thing that had ever

89

happened to her. Her breath hitched and she actually felt light-headed with the simple light contact of his lips against the back of her hand. Then, to her enjoyment, he turned her hand over and placed another kiss on the inside of her wrist, sending heat up her arm and all over her body.

"You smell so good," he said against her skin, then nibbled on her wrist. "Maybe I'm not so hungry after all." He pulled her closer.

"Oh, no." She pulled away playfully. "That food smells too good." He chuckled and tried to pull her closer, then nibbled on her neck as she held onto his shoulders. If someone had told her a year ago that her knees would get weak from someone just kissing her below her ear, she wouldn't have believed it.

During dinner, she looked at him across the small table and had never felt more nervous in her life. She tried to talk herself out of feeling that way. After all, she'd had sex before, plenty of times, with Travis. She didn't see what the big deal was. Although she liked to think she enjoyed it, half the time she'd just wished it would end. But Grant's kisses had awoken something in her that Travis never had. She knew there was a lot more to be experienced and wondered how much she didn't know when it came to romance. Would Grant see through her? Would he be able to tell that she still didn't quite know what men liked or wanted? She was pretty good at faking things. Maybe he wouldn't be able to tell.

She was so nervous that she hardly touched her plate. Grant frowned and asked, "Was there something wrong with the meal?"

She tried to smile and flirt her way out of answering the question, but Grant just looked at her, his eyes focused on her lips, waiting for the truth. She shrugged and sipped her tea, then blurted out.

"I'm nervous, okay?" She thought she could see understanding in his eyes as he leaned back in his chair. He almost looked like he was gloating.

"You?" His smile got even bigger. "You're nervous about what, exactly?"

She felt her face turning pink. "Us. You. This." She motioned with her hands towards the house.

He stood up quickly, then walked over and took her hands. Pulling her up next to him, he wrapped his arms around her waist. "I'm so glad." He kissed her softly on the lips. "If you weren't nervous, then it wouldn't mean as much."

"What?" She tried to pull back and look up into his eyes, but he shook his head and rested his forehead against hers.

"You aren't the only one that's nervous." His lips came back to hers in a slow, gentle kiss that made her knees shake. "You do something to me, always have." He started to nibble slowly down her neck. "You make me weak. Make me feel like I can't control myself." His mouth was leaving a hot trail down her body as his hands started running up her sides and back. "There is so much I want to say and do, but I've never had the guts to." He started walking them slowly backwards, towards the sliding glass door. "It's okay to be nervous." He pulled back and smiled at her. Then in one quick motion, he pulled her up into his arms as she squealed.

It was another first in her book. She'd never been carried to bed by a man who was about to make love to her. Her smile spread as she thought about all the excitement that had been hiding right in front of her for years. Grant was more than just the town's Goody Two-shoes. He was more complex than she'd ever imagined. Wrapping her arms around his neck, she held on to him as he walked in the house, making his way back to his room. She rained little kisses on his neck and nibbled on his ear as he went.

At one point, he stopped walking and took her mouth with his, causing her head to spin. Then he moved more quickly and his breath was more labored. His hands shook as he set her gently on the bed and looked down at her. "You're so beautiful. I can hardly believe that you're here with me."

She felt heat spread throughout when he looked at her like that. He stood next to the bed, then slowly put a knee next to her hip and hovered over her. His hand came up slowly, running his fingers down her cheek, her hair, her neck. She closed her eyes to the gentle touch. She'd never been treated like this before, like she was fragile. She wished he would speed up and just finish so these mixed feelings she was having would ease. Then he lay down next to her and started kissing her again, and she forgot all about speed. Instead, her mind was filled with what his mouth and hands were doing to her, consumed by him, only him, as he slowly undressed her, using skill she'd never experienced before. Little fires started on every inch of her skin he touched. Her knee came up as he ran his hands over her legs, hiking her skirt up until his hand rested on her thigh. Her fingers were holding onto his hair, but when he pulled away, her hands dropped to her sides.

His blue eyes were cloudy as she looked deep into them. His voice was coarse as he whispered to her, telling her how beautiful she was, how much he wanted her. Slowly, he reached up and started undoing the small buttons at the front of her dress, his eyes hungrily watching every inch of skin he exposed. When the front of her dress was completely opened, he pulled the two sides away to expose her skin. Her eyes closed as she felt his heated gaze on her bare skin. She couldn't have explained it if she'd tried, but just having Grant look at her like this caused her to feel something she'd never felt before.

"Please," she moaned as she looked up into his face. Reaching up, she took his face in her hands. "I need you."

He smiled as she tried to pull his shirt over his

head. He leaned back and quickly disposed of the shirt. "I want to enjoy every inch, every moment." His eyes heated as he continued to pull her dress down.

Her eyes explored his chest and arms. He was so tan and toned; she'd never imagined he'd look like this. She ran her fingers slowly over him until he stopped moving and closed his eyes. Pushing on his shoulders until he rolled onto his back, she came over him, straddling him with her legs over his hips. She felt his desire rub up against her core and moaned at the hardness and length. Her hands held her up so she hovered just above him. Her dress was hiked up, exposing her legs. Her top had been opened and she was fully exposed. Her lips were only inches above his, and she felt a little more in control. Then she closed her eyes and kissed him, his hands moved high on her legs. His coarse hands gently rubbed against her soft skin. His fingers played with the silk of her panties, played with the hem of the elastic until, finally, he pushed it aside and touched her bare skin.

Her hips jumped then started to pump with his movements as he continued to touch her. His kiss became more forceful as she moved above him. She felt her arms shake, then he quickly reversed their positions again, pausing to remove the rest of her clothes, then his own. Her smile faltered when she saw him standing next to the bed, fully ready for her. Part of her mind screamed that this wasn't going to work, that being with him shouldn't work. But something inside was determined beyond all reason, wanting him completely. He leaned over and pulled a condom from his nightstand, then came back next to her, running his eyes over every inch of her exposed skin.

When his hands ran gently down her side, she closed her eyes as his fingers once again found her sensitive skin. His mouth moved slowly over her chest from peak to peak as he lapped at her soft skin. Her fingers wrapped around his length and she smiled when she felt him jump in her hand, his entire body tensing as she stroked him slowly. She felt him shift, spreading her legs with his knees as he hovered above her, taking the kiss deeper than she could have imagined.

When he slid slowly into her, she felt something shift and knew that she never wanted the feeling to end, never wanted the moment to end. Her fingers dug into his hips and shoulders as his movements sped up. Her mind spun with the wonder, the feel of him filling her completely. She'd never experienced anything like it.

The feel, the smells, and the taste of him filled all of her senses until she felt complete. For the first time in her life, she knew what she wanted. She had never been more afraid than she was at that moment of discovery. Then he touched her bud as he moved inside her, and her whole world exploded as she died the sweetest death she'd ever experienced.

Grant felt Alex shiver with release, but he wasn't done with her yet. She wasn't getting off this easy, not after all the years of teasing him, of torturing him. Pulling her legs closer, he continued to move, her hips in his hands, as his mouth traveled over her skin, causing little bumps to form all over her. Her entire body was relaxed after her release, but he could feel her building again. Her hands had gone lax on the bed next to her body, but were now moving over his hips and butt, holding him to her, pulling him into her deeper. When she moaned his name, he kissed her until he, too, moaned with pleasure.

The tension in him transferred to her, and he could feel every inch of her burning with the same desire he felt. The slickness of their skin caused even more sensation as they moved over one another. She wrapped her legs around his hips, and he could feel himself building too fast. He wanted to slow down, to torture her, to keep her going. He wanted it to last forever, but when he felt her convulse around him again, he lost his own control and followed her. There was more power here than even he had expected, and when he rested his head next to her shoulder, he thought he felt his heart skip.

He lay there listening to their hearts beating

together and wondered what he'd have to do to convince her to stay the night. He felt their bodies cool and moved to pull a blanket over them. She groaned and tried to hold onto him. He chuckled. "I'm just covering us up. I left the window open and it feels like rain." He looked out the window and saw that the sun had gone down, and he realized that he'd totally lost track of time when he'd been with her. She snuggled up next to him, and he buried his face in her hair and took a deep breath of its soft scent. Her skin felt so soft as he ran his hands over her shoulders and arms. Her breasts were pushed up against his side, and he could feel every breath she took. Her long legs were wrapped around his. He closed his eyes, wishing they could stay like that forever.

"Can you stay?" he asked, placing a kiss on her hair.

"Hmmm." She snuggled closer to him and shook her head. "I'd better not. We start getting the cattle together tomorrow for auction. This time of year is busy." She turned her head and looked up at him. "If you have time, maybe you can swing by for lunch."

He thought about it. It was the beginning of fall and it was a busy time for him as well, especially since he had animals that needed tending and his father's business to start. "How about dinner instead?"

She looked down at him. "Fine, but this time I'll cook. Of course, you'll have to deal with my sisters and Chase." She frowned a little.

He ran his finger over her lips softly. "What's wrong?"

She shook her head. "Nothing. I guess I was just realizing that it's probably time for me to move out. Since..." She shook her head, then continued. "It's funny; I never realized how little privacy we actually have around there." She smiled at him. "It must drive Chase crazy."

Grant laughed. "I'll bet." He pulled her down and kissed her again. When they were both breathless again, he said, "Tell me you don't have to leave right away."

"Hmm, no." She shook her head and leaned back down for another kiss.

When she drove away two hours later, he stood out on the front porch and watched her car disappear. It started to rain and he felt the cold breeze hit him, cooling his skin but not what was inside. He was burning so hot for Alex that he was worried he was exposing himself too much to the pain that was bound to happen. After all, none of his other relationships had lasted long. But as he leaned back against the railing of his porch, he thought about all the ways this time was different. This was Alexis West, the first girl he'd ever kissed, the first and only girl he'd ever fallen for completely. He'd been infatuated with her since that day at the Grocery Stop when he'd caught her stealing. He smiled and turned to go back into his house, thinking of the differences between what they'd done back then and what they'd been doing for the last three hours.

It was just past midnight when the vehicle drove slowly by Grant's place. Seeing Alex's car, the driver gripped the steering wheel harder.

How dare that bitch do something like this? How dare she behave in such a humiliating way? She'd acted out at the diner, acting like a tramp, and Grant was part of it as well. Well, they needed to learn a lesson, and soon.

The car sped away, and thoughts of how to get back at the pair flashed behind the driver's angry eyes. Maybe there would be a perfect opportunity to show them how they were screwing everything up.

It wouldn't hurt to keep an eye out for ways to punish them for what they had done.

Jill Sanders

Chapter Seven

The next day was a bitch. The evening rain had cooled the morning off enough that there was a thick fog bank that had hindered his work in clearing a chunk of land. He planned to build a corral for his horses and goats, but first the trees and shrubs had to be cleared. Working in fog that was too thick to even see the end of your ax wasn't his idea of fun.

He had a small fire going, burning the shrubs and thistle. The thistle bushes had cut through his jeans several times, and he felt the blood drip down his thighs. By noon the fog had finally cleared off, and the heat was so overpowering, he stripped off his shirt as he worked. He ended up getting more scratches from the thorn bushes along the fence that lined his property, but by afternoon, he had cleared the entire area and was ready to start building the corral.

He walked back to his house, showered, and got ready for his dinner at Alex's place. His mind was so consumed with being with her that when he walked out to his truck, he didn't notice the flat tires until he was a foot away. Walking around his truck, he kicked each tire, noticing the large puncture marks in the sides of each of them.

"Damn it." He felt a headache coming on as he walked back into the house to call the sheriff. Then he called Alex to tell her he'd be late, but she told him she'd come right over instead. By the time the sheriff drove up, Alex's car was right behind his.

Everyone stood around his truck looking at the pierced tires and only one name came up.

"You know, Grant, there's nothing I can do, unless you have video of Travis doing this himself. Besides, his dad would have him out quicker than you could blink." The older man shook his head. "If you want, I'll drive you into town so you can get these fixed."

Grant looked at Alex, who nodded her head. "I'll help him with that. We have an old truck he can use until he gets new tires." Her arms were crossed over her blouse. She was wearing a flowered top with faded jeans and boots and looked beautiful. She looked like she'd spent the day in the fields, but even in the dusty clothes, she looked better somehow than she had in the dress she'd worn the night before. Maybe it was because she looked like she belonged in these clothes, like she was born to herd cattle all day.

He wrapped an arm around her as they watched the sheriff leave a few minutes later.

"I'm sorry about all this." She turned and wrapped her arms around him. "I don't understand why Travis is being a pain about all this. After all, he's the one who cheated." She frowned and pulled away a little, but he tightened his arms around her and pulled her closer.

"He's just acting up. He's always been that way." He shook his head and remembered plenty of times when Travis' temper had gotten the better of him. "He'll forget about it soon enough."

She sighed and he felt her relax a little. "Still, I'll help you pay…"

"Don't you dare." He pulled back. "You have no responsibility for his stupidity. Besides," he smiled, "insurance will pay for the tires. The loaner would help since it might be a few days before the truck will be fixed."

She smiled. "Sure thing. Let's get back. I'm dying for a shower and some food."

On the short drive back to Saddleback Ranch, they talked about their days. His day sounded like a walk in the park compared to hers. Herding cattle had always been a terrible job in his mind, but she talked about it as if she'd enjoyed every minute.

"I've always loved bringing the cattle in, helping separate them." She smiled over at him after parking her car next to the row of trucks by the barn. "You can borrow ol' Betty there." She

103

nodded towards an old blue truck that had been sitting there for as long as he could remember.

He laughed. "Does ol' Betty still run?"

She laughed with him. "She does, but you have to treat her real gentle." Alex purred and moved across the seat, almost getting into his lap. "Something tells me that won't be a problem for you." She ran her hands into his hair and pulled him down for a kiss that had his boots steaming. Then she was in his lap, straddling his hips, and he wished they were at his place again, instead of parked in front of her very full house.

"Alex?" He tried to pull away, but she was having none of it, her mouth fused to his.

"I couldn't stop thinking about you, about this, all day." She ran kisses along his jaw as his eyes closed. He thought about enjoying the feel of her for just another moment when they heard a cough outside the window. Both of them jumped to see Haley smiling at them.

"Well, well. Look at what we have here." Haley's arms were crossed over her chest as she stood outside the car, smiling.

Grant groaned and tried to move Alex off his lap, but then he realized that what she'd done to him was now in full view of Alex and her sister. His face turned a deep shade of red as the two of them laughed. Alex climbed out of her side of the car and walked with her sister towards the house, calling over her shoulder for Grant to go on to the back deck where Chase and Lauren were while she showered.

He took a few moments to calm down before stepping to the side of the house. When he did, he caught Lauren and Chase in a heated kiss and almost laughed as the two of them jumped apart. "I'm sorry," he apologized.

Chase just chuckled. "Don't worry, we're used to it. Living with Haley, there's a serious lack of privacy around here." Chase wrapped his arm around Lauren's shoulder.

"Alex mentioned something about your tires being slashed?" Lauren asked when Chase walked over to flip the burgers on the grill.

"Yeah." Grant sat down and told them what had happened. Lauren poured him a glass of ice tea as they talked. Alex walked out the back door half an hour later, freshly dressed in shorts, a halter top, and boots, one of her signature summer outfits that he'd always found very appealing.

By the time Haley walked out a few minutes later, the burgers were done. Grant had always had family dinners at his house; his parents had started the nightly ritual when he and his sister were living at home. But Alex's family had a level comfort with each other that he had never felt. Even Chase was now included in it. There were a couple dogs running around the yard, and after everyone was done eating, he and Chase walked off to toss a stick to them. The smaller dog, Buddy, had only three legs, but kept up with the Australian shepherd well enough.

"You know, if you had one of these, you might not have so many problems around your place," Chase said, tossing the stick again.

"One of what?" Grant looked up from scratching Buddy's ears.

"A dog." Chase laughed. "The McKay's have a two-year-old chocolate lab that had puppies last week. They are starting to look for homes for when the puppies are old enough." Chase smiled.

Grant thought about it for a second. "I don't know. I'm a little close to the road. It might be an issue."

Chase smiled and tossed the stick again. "You can train them. Actually, get Haley to work with it for a weekend and you'd be set." He nodded towards Haley, who was currently lying on a bench, napping. "She did wonders for Buddy."

"I suppose I can swing by the McKay's and take a look at them." Grant gave some serious thought to it the rest of the time they hung out with the dogs. It seemed he had one of every other kind of animal. Why not a dog at this point?

Just then Alex started walking towards them, and he forgot everything except her as he watched her hips sway. By the time she stopped in front of him, his mouth had gone completely dry.

"Well, I'll just go help my wife..." Chase

excused himself quickly.

"Want to go for a walk?" Alex took his hand in hers and tugged him towards the side of the house. They walked, holding hands in silence across the fields until they reached an old oak that had a large swing on a low branch. Alex sat down and Grant pushed her, watching her hair blow in the breeze.

"I've never given serious thought to leaving this place," she said out of the blue.

"Why would you? It's perfect." He smiled, looking across the field as the fading sun rested on the white house, causing it to almost glow in the dying light.

"It is, isn't it?" She sighed. He stopped pushing her and walked around, holding the ropes in his hand until the swing stopped.

"Are you thinking of leaving?" he asked as he looked down at her.

She shook her head. "I was for a while, then..." She looked up at him and shook her head again. "No, I'm staying." She smiled.

"I've been to a lot of places the last few years. Traveling is exciting, but knowing you can come back here..." He turned and nodded towards the house. A distant laugh could be heard from the back of the house. The sound of the dogs barking with joy and the cattle lowing in the distant fields made the place seem like home. He shook his head. "It's the reason I came back." He turned back towards her.

She stood and wrapped her arms around his shoulders. "I'm so glad you did." Then she kissed him. He walked her backwards a few steps until her back was up against the tree trunk as he took the kiss deeper, his hands roaming over her smooth skin until he felt he couldn't control himself any longer. But her hands were wrapped around him, holding him tight to her. He desperately wished they were anywhere but standing in an open field. Then her hands went to his jeans, and his mind went blank as she started rubbing him through his jeans.

"I want you. I haven't stopped thinking about you since last night," he said against her skin. "God help me, if you don't stop"—he took hold of her hands to still them and end the torture—"I'll end up taking you right here in the open field, not caring who sees or hears us." He took a couple deep breaths to steady himself.

"I don't care." She smiled up at him, then pulled him a few feet behind the tree and lay down in the tall grass. "Make love to me here, Grant. Under this tree, as the stars come out." He followed her to the ground; he couldn't have stopped himself if he wanted. Her arms and legs wrapped around him as he came next to her. She was pulling his clothes off quickly, and his own hands shook as he tried to gently remove hers. She was moving too fast, he couldn't control his need much longer if she kept this pace up. Then she was pushing him over, straddling his hips, moving against him, trailing kisses down his chest until she reached the hem of his jeans. Then she was pulling them over his hips. When she took him into her mouth, his shoulders bounded off the ground, and he bit his lip on a groan. His hands went to her hair as she used her mouth to please him.

When he reversed their positions, he looked down at her. She had a wicked smile on her face. "You think this is funny?" His voice was hoarse.

She nodded and wiggled underneath him. In one quick motion, he yanked her shorts down and had a finger in her heat, causing her to gasp and moan. Tossing her head back, she bit her bottom lip and dug her fingers into the grass, holding herself still. When he dipped his head and tasted her soft skin, she squealed and grabbed his head, holding him to her core. His fingers moved slowly in and out of her as he used his tongue on the tight little nub he found. When he felt her convulse and tasted her sweetness on his tongue, he eased up and slid slowly into her.

She wrapped her arms and legs around him, holding on as they rocked together as the sun set behind them, casting shadows over them.

When the stars were out, they lay tangled together and watched the dark skies, talking about their hopes and dreams. He'd never felt more connected to anyone in his entire life.

They finally dressed again and made their way back towards the barn. Alex kissed him goodnight and gave him the truck keys. As he drove home in ol' Betty, he thought of a plan to get Alex to stay with him at his place. At least until he could convince her to marry him.

It was so funny to watch Grant drive up to his house in the old blue truck. Then realization dawned. It was the West's old truck.

Shooting out his tires had given a little pleasure, but not enough. Maybe there was something else that could be done to discourage them from being so humiliating. After all, the whole town knew that they were seeing each other now. Maybe the game needed to be stepped up some more? Maybe it was time to face one of them and show them how their actions were ruining everything?

Maybe attacking Grant in his wallet would be the best method? So many possibilities...Which one to choose?

The next day Alex woke late. She didn't

normally mind, but today she was due at Mama's for the early shift. Jamella wasn't a tyrant boss, but she did always make whoever was late take the trash out at the end of their shift. Alex hated hauling the trash out, so she was almost never late.

When she arrived, she got the stink eye from Jamella, but quickly picked up her tables and got to work. She didn't really know what had driven her to get the job in the first place other than needed a little extra gas money. Maybe it had been seeing Lauren struggling to pay the electric bill that year. Whatever it was, she'd quickly gotten addicted to working there. The work wasn't backbreaking, but it was still work. She had learned to deal with the drudgery; what she was addicted to was seeing and interacting with the people. Some people in town she loved to catch up with, others not so much. It was around noon when Savannah and her crowd of lemmings walked in. They were greeted by several older ladies who ran charity events around town. The local paper was always filled with the details and pictures of anything the ladies did. Sometimes it felt like every time they sneezed, it was included. But when Haley's cow had won the county fair last year, there wasn't a word printed in the local papers about it. Lauren had been so upset about it, she'd taken a full-page ad out herself just to show the town how great her sister was.

Alex pasted on her best smile and walked over to take orders. Savannah had made sure to sit on the very inside of the booth, far away from any falling food this time. When Alex walked into the back to place the orders, she realized that Savannah had actually done her a favor. If she was still with Travis, she wouldn't feel so free, and she wouldn't be with Grant. And if there was one thing she now knew, it was that she wanted to be with Grant as long as she could.

Being with him was the most fun she'd had in years. Not only was the physical relationship a million times better that it had been with Travis, Grant actually listened to her when she talked. He treated her like she was someone to be cherished, like she was smart. She still couldn't get over how much they already knew about one another. It helped that he'd always been around the ranch when they were younger. She'd just always overlooked him, and he'd always treated her like a sister. Or so she'd thought.

When she carried out the group's order, everyone all of a sudden got very quiet. She knew they'd been talking about her; it was written all over their guilty faces. She pasted on a smile and delivered their food, wishing they would hurry up and choke it down and leave. But instead the older women left, leaving the three younger ones and Savannah behind.

When she approached them with their ticket, Savannah sneered at her. "I don't think so, Alexis. It cost me four hundred dollars to have my dress cleaned up from the last time I was in here." She looked down at her nails and smiled. "You'll just have to dock it from your pay."

Alex set the bill down, then crossed her arms over her chest. "Savannah, I suspect you can read."

Savannah's eyes got real big. "Of course I can. What kind of statement is that?"

Alex nodded towards the sign over the door. "You know Ma's rules. '*Either you pay, or you clean. One way or another, the bill is gonna be paid.*'" Alex walked away with a smile.

She'd just walked into the back when she heard the commotion out front. Looking through the window, she saw Jamella grab Savannah's arm and stop her from walking out.

"Now girl, I know'd you are smarter than dat. I heard Alex warn you. You either pay dat bill, or I'll call your folks. Better yet, da police." Savannah's friends all left when Jamella grabbed her.

"Jamella, you know full well that Alexis ruined my new dress last time I was in here. She's your employee and therefore responsible to pay that bill."

"Dat between you and her. In Mama's, if you eat da food, you pay for it. Now, are you gonna pay or shall I…" Jamella reached for the phone.

"Fine, but see if I ever step foot in this establishment again." Savannah's eyes darted around to find Alex smiling back at her.

When Jamella walked into the back, a huge smile on her face, she mumbled, "See if I let dat skinny girl back in here. Suits me just right if'n dat girl never come back."

The rest of her shift, Alex felt lighthearted and free. By the end of the night, she felt like she'd won the war with Savannah. She knew that people would talk about what had happened. After all, the small town didn't usually have a lot to gossip about. Since her breakup with Travis had made the list of top stories of the year, anything to do with it was sure to spread fast.

It was past seven when she walked out to dump the trash in the bin. She paused momentarily when she saw Travis smoking as he leaned against his truck in the parking lot. Leaving the back diner door opened, she straightened her spine and walked past Travis to toss the trash into the dumpster. When she tried to walk past him again, he grabbed her arm and pulled her to a stop.

"What do you mean causing all this trouble?" His voice was low and his words a little slurred. He flicked his cigarette butt. He was probably drunk. Sniffing, she smelled the booze on him past the cigarette smells.

"Let go of my arm, Travis." She tried to pull herself free, only to be spun around and shoved against his truck.

"I'll let you go when I want to. Now answer my question." He shook her arm and leaned closer to her, his breath hitting her face. Cigarettes and cheap beer. How had she ever allowed this man to kiss her, smelling like that? Her stomach rolled.

"I don't know what you're talking about." She said louder, hoping Willard would hear. When he didn't budge, she pushed at his chest and said, "Travis Nolan, let go of me right now."

"Why do you have the sheriff coming over to the house? I didn't do nothing. Besides, whatever's happening to Grant Do-gooder, he deserves it."

His fingers were digging into her arm and she felt his door handle biting into her hip. "You leave Grant alone. You're the one who cheated." She pushed him again, only to have him come up closer and pin her body against his truck with his. Her hands were pinned between them and she started to panic. Then she remembered what her pa had taught her and she used all her strength to step on his foot and yank her knee up to hit him in his crotch.

When he doubled over, she rushed towards the back door, calling out behind her. "You leave Grant out of this." She stopped just inside the door and looked back. She was satisfied when she saw that he was still hunched over, grabbing his crotch. "Just let it go, Travis." Then she shut the door and leaned her head against the cool metal.

"You handled dat well." Alex jumped at Jamella's voice behind her. When she looked, she saw Jamella standing there with a huge frying pan in her hands. "Dat boy come around here again, he get the heavy end of dis." She patted the pan and

115

smiled as Alex laughed.

Chapter Eight

It had taken Grant three days to get the wood fence up for the corral. The heavy boards were strong enough to keep even a charging bull in. He stood back and smiled as he felt the cool air coming across the fields. They were in for some more rain, and he was glad he'd gotten the work done before it came. It looked like everything was finally falling into place; he'd even gotten his truck back earlier that morning.

He turned and watched as his parents' car pulled in front of his house. His father stepped out and waved as Grant walked towards him and shook his hand.

"Looking good, son." His father nodded towards the corral. "You did a fine job." He slapped him on the back.

"Thanks. What brings you out this way?" His

parents frequently visited his place. His mother always brought him food or pies, and his father came out to lend a helping hand when he could. But something told Grant that his father was out here for reasons other than a social visit. His father's smile fell away.

"Well…" They both looked to the sky when it started to rain lightly. "Let's head up to the porch so we don't get soaked."

They walked up the stone steps together. "Do you want a beer?" When his father shook his head and sat down in one of his porch chairs, Grant knew it was serious.

"I hate to tell you this, but it seems like someone has filed a complaint against you to the Texas Bar. They claim you haven't filed your MCLE hours and want the state to revoke your license." His father held up his hand. "Now, before you get all gung ho, I've already filed an appeal."

He stood up, ready to fight. "Damn it Dad, we filed those last month. They aren't due for another few weeks." He thought about how this would delay their business plans and felt the anger grow.

"I know, I know." His father stood up and put a hand on his shoulder. "It's a scare tactic. Seems to me that someone in power around here wants you out of town. Or at least out of a job." His father winked at him. "Don't worry, not even the mayor has the power to take away your license. But he does have enough power to make us jump through a few hoops." His father frowned, and patted him on the back again. "Is she worth it?"

"She is." He smiled when his father laughed and nodded.

"Good." His father smiled back at him.

After his father drove away, Grant showered and dressed, then decided to swing by Saddleback Ranch and see what Alex was up to.

When he got there, she was just parking in front of the barn herself. He smiled and pulled ol' Betty back into her spot.

"Hi." She smiled and walked over to the truck.

"Hi, I'm just bringing the ol' girl back." He shut the door and pulled Alex into his arm and placed a soft kiss on her lips. "Thanks," he said when he pulled back.

Her eyebrows shot up. "For the kiss?" She smiled and wrapped her arms tighter around his neck.

He laughed. "For the loan. I got my truck back earlier today."

She smiled. "Any time. Have you had dinner?"

"Yes, but I wouldn't mind a little more dessert." He leaned in and was hovering just above her lips when they both heard a cough. Haley stood just outside the barn doors, with a large smile on her face. Grant pulled back but wrapped an arm around Alex, holding her close.

119

"Heard you gave Travis what he deserved today," Haley said, walking by them. "It's about time."

Grant watched Haley head towards the house. He turned to Alex and looked down at her. "What did she mean by that?"

Alex looked after her sister with a frown. "It means that Haley has a big mouth, and Jamella can't keep anything from my sisters."

Grant turned her slightly. He noticed a dark bruise high on her left arm. "Did Travis do that to you?" He dropped his arms and looked into her eyes.

She shrugged and smiled a little. "I'm sure it's nothing compared to how his balls look now." Grant felt his blood begin to boil. When he looked at her arm, he could see the ring around it where Travis' hand had been. He knew Alex was fragile, and he'd been raised to never raise a hand to a woman. Hell, he'd never even been in a real fight. But his mind was flashing images of beating the shit out of Travis at the moment.

"Listen…" She stepped closer to him, taking his mind off images of him standing over Travis' unconscious body. Then she took his shirt in her hands gently, trying to pull him closer. "I handled him. It's not the first time he's been a little rough with me. This time I had no reason not to retaliate." She smiled.

His heart was pounding hard in his chest, and

he felt like bashing Travis' face in. But she looked up at him with those chocolate eyes, and he couldn't help but being proud of how she'd handled Travis all by herself. "If he comes around again, give me a call." He leaned his forehead against hers.

"Sure." She smiled at him, then she wrapped her arms around his neck again and whispered, "What do you say you come upstairs and help me wash my back?"

His mind flashed to images of Alex wet, slick, and naked. A smile flew to his lips so fast he couldn't stop it. Then he heard a screen door slam shut somewhere, and he blinked the image away.

"I'd love to, but your place is a little too crowded at the moment." They heard the dogs barking, and Haley and Lauren laughing.

"I suppose you're right." She sighed. "I could grab a bag and drive you home?" She leaned back in to him.

"I'd like that." He placed a kiss on her lips, quickly.

When she turned and rushed into the house, she called over her shoulder, "I'll just be a few minutes."

He stood there and watched her go, feeling excited. Then he heard another cough behind him. Turning, he saw Chase leaning against the fence a few feet away.

"It's damn hard to get any privacy around here." Chase smiled.

Grant walked over to him and shook his hand.

Chase nodded towards ol' Betty. "Looks like you've got everything fixed again."

"Yeah." Grant put his foot up on the bottom rung of the fence and watched an older gray horse in the corral. "Sounds like Travis decided to approach Alex today instead of sneaking around my property."

"What?" Chase leaned up, looking like he was ready for a fight.

"She's okay." Grant looked off towards the house. "Kicked him where it counts." He laughed and looked back at Chase. "But, if I were you, I'd keep an eye out around here. Travis likes sneaking around."

"That son of a..." Chase said, and then started pacing.

"Exactly." Grant smiled and relaxed against the fence, knowing Chase would make sure everything was secure and protected around the ranch.

By the time Alex drove him up his driveway, his mind was on one thing only. Her.

When they walked into his place, he didn't give her a chance to talk. Instead, he pulled her close to him and walked her backwards towards his room as he rained kisses along her neck, nibbling his way down to her shoulders. By the time they made it to the bedroom, they were both naked, their clothes leaving a trial from the front door. He didn't stop in the bedroom. Instead, he walked her back until they hit the shower wall. He reached over and turned on the spray, not really registering the cold water until he felt her shiver in his arms.

"Oh, sorry." He chuckled, then turned on the hot water. He grabbed a handful of shampoo and started rubbing it into her hair and down her body until she was moaning and holding onto the sides of his shower. Turning her until she faced away from him, he used his soapy hands to wash her hair and back. "I like your hair this length. Of course it was nice shorter too, but this seems to fit you better." Her hair was so soft as it ran down to the middle of her back. She moaned and placed her palms against the shower wall, holding herself up. He continued to roam his hands lower, over her ribs and her narrow waist, until he reached her perfect bottom. He leaned closer, his chest hitting her back as he reached around and ran his fingers over her hips, pulling her against him.

"Please," she moaned and leaned her head back against his shoulder.

He smiled. "I never thought I'd have Alexis West begging me in my shower," he said softly into her ear. He felt her shiver as she reached around and tried to pull his hips closer. He pulled back for just a moment, long enough to slip on the condom he'd been lucky enough to think of grabbing before they'd entered the shower. Then he was pulling her back towards him.

"Here, put your foot up on the seat." He helped her move her right foot up, then she leaned forward as he ran his eyes over her. She was perfect. She had a little freckle on her right cheek, and he ran his finger over it, smiling. Then she arched her back and he forgot everything except for the need to be inside her.

It was another first for Alex. She'd never made love in a shower before, or standing up, for that matter. She smiled to herself and arched her back. The anticipation was almost too much. She felt her legs quiver as she waited for him to touch her again.

Then his hands were lightly on her bottom and her hips as he held her still and slowly entered her. She moaned. He filled her completely as she tried to grip the slick walls of the shower. His hands pulled her back towards him as he thrust deeper into her. She closed her eyes, letting the water run over her, enjoying the motion as he slowly drove her crazy, building her up.

"My god," he said, then turned her a little so she could hold onto the built-in shelf that held his bottles of shampoo. She gripped it tightly, holding on as he moved faster. His slick hands reached around, running over every inch of her, causing her nipples to pucker into his palms. Then he leaned over and whispered in her ear, telling her how good she felt, and she felt herself convulse around him, screaming out his name.

She felt like she was drowning. Her head was under the spray, and water poured down the back of her head and into her eyes and nose.

Grant pulled her up and away from the water, then turned her around as the water was shut off. He grabbed a towel and gently started drying her. She smiled. "I could get used to this kind of treatment."

"Good." He smiled down at her and continued to rub her skin, softly. Then when he was satisfied, he quickly dried his chest and legs. She watched every movement. He was tan and toned, and when she reached out to touch his chest, she realized every part of him was hard. Smiling, she walked closer to him and wrapped her arms around him as he tossed the towel on the countertop.

She laughed as he picked her up and carried her into his bedroom. "I could definitely get used to this." She kissed his neck just under his ear and heard him growl a little.

Then he set her down on the bed and covered her again. "Where were we?" he asked as he settled between her legs. "Oh, I think I remember now." He slid into her slowly again, and her hips rolled up to meet his thrusts. Then he was leaning in and kissing her, and her body felt like it was spinning out of control. His hands roamed over her sides, over her legs, pulling them up closer to her chest until she felt him completely inside with every thrust.

Her fingernails dug into his hips and his tight butt as she tried to match every stroke. Her breath was hitching and she felt like there were goose bumps rising all over her body. Still, she wrapped her legs around his hips and held on until she felt herself melt around him as he held himself still over her.

When he collapsed, he made sure to move to the side so he wouldn't crush her, another thing she enjoyed about him. He was so thoughtful and considerate. She smiled up at the ceiling and started to mentally list the reasons Grant was so much better for her than Travis had been. She'd made it up to twenty-four when his hand moved over her hip and she lost her train of thought.

He pulled her close and snuggled into her hair. "Now you smell like me." He laughed.

"What?" She blinked a few times while trying to understand him.

"The shampoo." He leaned up and looked down at her. "I like the smell of yours better. It's softer, sexier." He leaned in and sniffed. "Yup, all I smell is me." He frowned. "Maybe you can bring some of your stuff over here, so if we end up doing that again, I'll get to smell you instead." He smiled at her.

She laughed. "You are so funny." She sat up and looked back at him. "If you'll retrieve my bag from the front hallway, you might just get to smell *me*."

He jumped up and grabbed her bags. She went into the bathroom, closing him out as she quickly rinsed off again, this time using her own shampoos and conditioners. She even went as far as spraying herself with her body spray. Then she donned her sexiest underwear, put a silk shirt and a jean skirt on, and walked out to see him eating a bowl of cereal in bed. He looked just like a kid stuck at home watching cartoons. She laughed at him.

"What?" He looked up at her and smiled. "You know, I had plans of taking you out somewhere soon." He frowned. "Of course, maybe we'll plan that for when we can drive into Tyler, since Mama's is really the only place in town for food."

"I'd like that." She came and sat next to him. He was wearing his jeans, no socks and no shirt, and he looked damn sexy. She leaned over and looked into the bowl. "Is that Fruity Pebbles?"

He smiled. "Yup, you'd be surprised at how healthy these things are."

She laughed. "Really?"

"Do you want some?" He held out his bowl. "I think there's an old movie on tonight." He patted the spot next to him. She sat next to him and took a bite of his cereal.

"Cold cereal and an old movie sounds good." She took another bite. "You know, it's been a long time since I had cereal in bed while watching TV." She smiled as the Wizard of Oz came on.

"I love this movie." Grant took a bite of the cereal. His eyes were glued to the set and Alex felt her heart shift for a man who ate cereal in bed while watching one of her favorite movies ever.

Later that night, as she was getting ready to drive home, he pulled her close and kissed her until her toes curled.

"What do you say to going out with me to The Rusty Rail next Thursday?" he asked as they stood on his front deck. Thursday nights were karaoke nights at the Rusty Rail, the only bar and dance place in town. Alex always loved going to the Rusty Rail, but hadn't been there since her break up with Travis.

"Sounds good." She knew it was time to show everyone in town that she'd moved on. Even the prospect of seeing Travis with Savannah didn't shake her like it would have if she wasn't going to be with Grant.

While she drove home, she thought of her time with Grant and, for once, her future actually looked good. She still may not know what it was she wanted to do or be in life, but she knew she was going to enjoy every moment of their time together.

When she walked in the front door, it was just

past midnight. Every light was off in the house except for Haley's. She knocked lightly on her sister's door and went in when her sister answered.

"Hey." Alex walked in and sat at the end of her sister's bed. Haley was sitting on top of her comforter, a book in hand, her long, dark hair tied back with a twist. Lauren and Haley had been blessed with their father's green eyes. It wasn't that Alex didn't like having their mother's brown eyes. She just wished she could remember more of her mother so she could see it when she looked in the mirror.

"Just getting home?" Haley set her book down and smiled. "We took bets if you were going to stay the night. Looks like I won." Her sister crossed her arms over her chest, a satisfied smile on her lips.

Alex tilted her head. "Seriously? Why would I stay there? I've never spent the night with Travis."

"Yeah, but…" Haley scooted closer to her sister and laid a hand on her knee. "Grant is no Travis."

Her sister was right. The only reason she'd never stayed the night with Travis was that she'd actually wanted to be home instead of wrapped in his arms. She wanted to stay at Grant's, snuggled up next to him, waking up in his arms.

"Earth to Alex." Haley shook her knee, causing her to blink and realize she'd been daydreaming about being with Grant.

"Sorry, I guess I'm a little more tired than I

thought." Alex rubbed her eyes and yawned.

"Sure you are." Haley smiled and winked.

Alex got up and walked to the door. "Good night."

"Alex." Haley waited until she turned back. "Next time, stay. You won't regret it."

That night, Alex had a hard time getting to sleep. Her body was worn out from the long day at work and the hours of making love with Grant, but her mind just refused to shut down.

She kept running over lists. Lists of how Grant was different, better than Travis. She wondered why her mind was feeling unsettled about taking the next step with Grant. It wasn't as if she was moving in with him. They'd been together a few times now, and they were enjoying each other. She knew Grant would never cheat on her. There was no way Mr. Goody Two-shoes would do anything like that, even if he had changed a lot since she'd used the nickname for him. He was still Grant underneath, and she knew he wasn't capable of something like that.

He was kinder and more caring than anyone she'd ever dated. He walked her to her car, opened the doors, and always leaned in and kissed her, telling her to drive safe on the way home. She smiled and turned over in bed, trying to get more comfortable. She wished he had a cell phone, so she could text him, but she knew he was putting off getting a phone. Maybe she would just swing by and pick one up for him. It could be an early birthday present.

She sat up in bed and gasped. She didn't even know his birthday. She rushed to her bookshelves and searched through her yearbooks. Pulling out one after another, she saw picture after picture of him, but none of them showed his birth date. Feeling frustrated, she walked over to her laptop and flipped it open. She knew he didn't really get into technology, but maybe it was out there somewhere on the web.

She pulled up Facebook and was shocked to see a picture of him and a dark-skinned girl smiling at the camera on what appeared to be his personal Facebook page. She relaxed when she remembered what he'd said about his ex, Terry. So, this was the kind of girl he'd dated? She looked at the dark-haired beauty. Her dark curly hair hung past her shoulders, and her skin glowed in the sunlight. Alex flipped through a few more pictures. There were only a dozen, but she stared at each one, taking in every detail of his transformation from chunky Grant with glasses to hunky Grant with a well-toned body. There was a picture of Grant with another man, a large bodybuilder type who looked a great deal like Terry. She realized it must be Sam. She felt a little sad looking at the pictures of the three of them. She could tell Grant had really looked up to the man, and she wished she'd had the opportunity to meet him. Then she looked at his sister, Terry, and wondered what she'd gone through, losing her only sibling.

Taking a chance, she used Google to search Grant's name. Narrowing down the search, she typed in Fairplay and was shocked when a professional website came up: Holton Legal Advice. She clicked into it and saw an image of Grant and his father. The site looked new since some of the links weren't up and running yet, but from what she could tell, they were running an online business to help people file simple legal paperwork such as wills. She spent almost an hour going through the website. By the time she shut down her computer, she knew several things more about Grant, including that his birthday was less than a month away. Perfect. She could drive into Tyler and buy him a new cell phone and have a wonderful excuse. After all, with an online business like that, he needed to be connected.

Closing her laptop, she jumped back into bed with a smile on her face. She was going to buy Grant a cell phone, and the next time she went over to his place, she was going to spend the whole night with him.

Chapter Nine

By the end of the week, word had spread throughout town of the little scene behind Mama's. When people walked into the diner, they either smiled or chuckled at her. She'd known for some time that the small town had a thing for gossiping about her, and she'd never shied away from it before. This time she wished people would just leave her alone.

She hadn't seen Travis or Savannah in a while, and she hadn't really heard any gossip about the two of them either. It was almost as if they weren't really an item. People in town knew why she'd broken off the engagement, and they also knew that she was currently seeing Grant. But for the most part, most of the gossip around town was about what she'd done to the two of them.

She had hoped that with the county fair starting at the end of the month, people would have found

Jill Sanders

something else to talk about and the gossip would have died down a little. But on several occasions that day at the diner, she'd overheard her name and had turned to see someone laugh or chuckle at the story that was being told.

By the time she drove up the long driveway at the ranch, she was beat and it wasn't even noon yet. She'd made it halfway up the drive when she spotted Lauren walking next to her horse, Tanner. At first she thought about just slowing down and waving then continuing up the drive, but her sister shocked her by hunching over and throwing up.

Alex hit the brakes and rushed to her sister's side. "What is it? Are you alright?" She held her sister's hair back as she continued to throw up all over her own boots. Then Lauren leaned up and gave her a weak smile. Alex reached over and felt her sister's forehead. "Oh, honey, you're sick. I'll go get Chase."

"No!" Lauren grabbed her arm, stopping her. "I'm fine. I'll be okay." She smiled and took a water bottle from her saddlebag and rinsed her mouth.

"Lauren, you probably have heat stroke or something. You know better than to…" Lauren interrupted her by laughing. "What?" Alex felt like stomping her foot in frustration. Lauren never thought about herself. Her older sister had always given up everything she'd wanted for Alex and Haley. She'd probably worked out in the sun all day since sunrise and, knowing her, hadn't eaten

134

much or taken any breaks. Alex mentally thought about tattling on her to Chase. After all, she'd seen a huge change in her sister since the pair had let everyone know last year that they'd married almost eight years ago.

"What?" Alex dropped her hand that was still on her sisters. "What's so funny?"

"You. This." Lauren motioned around the field, then towards the house. "Me. Chase. Everything." Alex stood in shock as her sister turned in circles, hugging herself as she laughed.

"Okay, definitely heat stroke. I'm taking you home right now." She grabbed for her sister's arm.

"Alex." Lauren took her by the shoulders and smiled at her. "It's not heat stroke. I'm pregnant. Or at least I think I am." Her sister's smile got bigger as she waited for the words to sink in.

Alex's mind stopped. Her vision actually grayed around the edges so that all she could see was Lauren's face. Her sister's sea green eyes almost glowed in the sunlight. Her dark hair blew in the light breeze and her cheeks were a dark pink. A baby! Lauren was having a baby. Chase and Lauren were having a baby.

Then she grabbed Lauren by the shoulders and pulled her into a hug so strong that by the time she let go, tears were falling down both of their faces. "A baby?" Alex smiled at her sister. "You're having a baby?"

Lauren nodded her head with a smile. "I think

135

so. I took a test and it said positive. Besides, I'm late and you know that whole thing about morning sickness. Well, for me, it's evening sickness. I've been sick the last three evenings in a row. By the time dinner time rolls around I feel better. I've been sneaking out here the last two nights with Tanner to get out of letting Chase know what's going on. I'm a coward."

"Why?" Alex stepped back and frowned. "Don't you want Chase to know? Doesn't he want kids?" she asked.

Lauren quickly shook her head. "Oh, no. He absolutely wants children. We've been trying since he moved in last year. It's just…"

Alex smiled. "You wanted to be sure first?"

"Exactly." Lauren grabbed her sister's hand and started walking with her and Tanner towards Alex's car. "Now that I'm almost positive, I want to tell him in a special way."

Alex smiled. "I can help you out there." She stopped by her car and leaned in to grab her cell phone. "Leave everything to me." She punched a few buttons and made some calls. By the time she hung up, Lauren and Chase had the most romantic place in town all to themselves that night. A few close friends had dropped everything without any questions and had made themselves available to help out.

At eight that night, Alex had Chase drive her into town under the pretense that she'd forgotten something at the diner and had such a headache that she couldn't see well enough to drive. It in part was true, since she'd spent almost three hours preparing the surprise. Her new brother-in-law hadn't complained about the drive. Instead, he'd helped load her into his truck and had driven her the ten minutes into town.

"Maybe you can run in and get my purse. It's just behind the counter. Jamella said she'd leave the front door unlocked for me since she closed up early today. She might be in the back, but..." She signed and leaned her head against the glass. "I'm seeing double right now." She closed her eyes to emphasize it a little more. When she heard him sigh, she almost chuckled. No doubt he was thinking of how he'd look carrying a woman's purse back across Main Street. But then the car door opened, and he darted out in the light rain that had started falling. He ran across the street and in through the front door of the dark diner.

Quickly getting out, Alex rushed to the back door and watched with Jamella and Willard from the kitchen window as Chase stood motionless inside the front door.

Lauren stood in front of a small table, right in the middle of the dining room. White candles lit the entire room, making the boring diner look like the most romantic spot in town. A cream-colored tablecloth covered the round table, and white flowers and rose petals covered almost every inch of it and the floor.

"What?" she heard Chase say. Then he smiled and walked slowly forward. They watched as he pulled Lauren into a deep kiss. "This is a nice surprise." He pulled back.

"I hope you like it," Lauren said in a soft voice.

"I love it." He looked around, then a small frown formed on his face. "But why? Our anniversary isn't until the spring. It's not my birthday, or yours." He smiled a little.

"Well, it's…" She watched her sister's shoulders rise and fall. "It's just that I took a test today and I passed."

Chase's eyebrows shot up. "Test?"

Lauren nodded. "A pregnancy test."

Alex watched Chase's face from across the room. Everyone was peeking out the window, holding their breath. They all jumped a little when Chase let out a large "Whoop" and then rushed over, picked Lauren up off her feet, and swung her around several times.

Laughing, Jamella whispered. "Let's leave them to their moment. We have work to do." She pushed on Willard's arm and patted Alex's hand.

Grant showed up a few minutes later dressed in a black suit and looking damn sexy. "Why did I have to wear this and come down here?" He pulled at his tie and frowned a little. "And why did I have to come in the back way?" He looked a little irritated.

"Because..." She grabbed his arm and tugged him towards the window and pointed out front where Chase and Lauren were dancing. "They're having a baby and we're serving them dinner." She motioned towards the kitchen where they were working hard making wonderful food. Willard and Jamella had pulled out all the stops tonight.

Grant looked out the window at Chase and Lauren as they danced slowly in the dimly lit room, swaying to music playing from the old jukebox. His sour face turned soft and by the time he turned back to her, there was a large smile on his face.

"Really?" He nodded to the open window. "They're having a kid?"

She smiled and nodded, wrapping her arms around his neck as he pulled her closer.

Just then Haley rushed in. Her hair was in tangles and her shirt was partially untucked. "Where are they? Am I late?"

"What happened to you?" Alex pulled back and frowned at her sister.

"Flat tire," she said as she tucked in her shirt.

"That's the second one this week." Alex frowned.

"I know. Chase told me to replace all four tires the first time, but..." She trailed off and shrugged her shoulders.

"They weren't cut were they?" Grant started to

139

walk towards Haley.

"No, just old and bald." Haley smiled. "Am I late?" She rushed to the window and peeked out. "Oh, look at them." Haley smiled, then turned to Alex. "We're having a baby!" It came out a little loud, and they heard Lauren and Chase laugh from the front room.

Less than a minute later, Chase walked through the swinging door. "Everyone might as well come out front. We can hear you all back here, anyway." He chuckled.

"Oh no," Alex grabbed Haley's arm as she started walking towards the door to head out front. "This is your night, just the two of you. I mean"—she smiled—"the three of you now."

"What if it's the four of them?" Haley asked, earning a pinch on the arm from Alex. "I'm just saying…," she whispered.

"Go on out there. We'll bring your food in a minute," Alex said, pushing Chase out the door. Then she turned to everyone in the kitchen. "Okay, we're going to make this a night they won't forget."

Two hours later, Alex looked over at Grant and smiled. "It was perfect, wasn't it?" She leaned on the table, looking across it at Grant. He'd removed his tie and unbuttoned the first few buttons of his white shirt. His dress coat was flung over the back of the chair, which he sat backwards in.

He smiled at her and her heart skipped a little. "Yeah, you have a real talent for putting events together." He reached over and took her hand.

Everyone had left for the night except Willard, who was still in the back cleaning up. After Lauren and Chase had left, there had been enough food left over that Grant and Alex had sat down to a quiet meal themselves. Alex considered it their first real date. The lights were low and the music was softly playing. Grant looked extremely handsome in his suit, and she was wearing one of her favorite dresses. She smiled across at him.

"Speaking of putting things together..." She leaned on the table tilting her head a little. "Why didn't you tell me you were starting an online business with your father?"

He rolled his eyes and groaned, then took another swig of his beer. "Because it's not up and running yet. It was just an idea I ran by my father years ago on the phone. I didn't know he would hire a company to pull it all together." He smiled. "It does look good though."

"I think it's a wonderful idea." She smiled as he leaned forward a little more.

"Really?" he asked.

"Well, sure. I mean, just think of how many online users there are that need simple things like help updating their wills." She sighed. "I think it's a very smart plan. Maybe I can help out."

He shook his head then smiled as he held out his hand. Just then there was a large crash as glass from the front window of the diner sprayed over the both of them. Grant quickly tucked Alex's body behind his, but not before glass shards flew into her face and hair.

Oh, what fun that had been. It had felt so good to hear the glass shatter. To feel the adrenaline. To hear and see the destruction. Maybe this was the key? Maybe now they would stop?

If not, there were other ideas. Other plans. Other ways to prove to them that they had screwed everything up. Besides, it was too much fun to stop now.

The headlights hit the white line as the car headed down the street towards Grant's place. Why stop now? A smile slowly spread. There was so much more to destroy. After all, they'd be busy for a while. There was plenty of time for a little more destruction.

Grant held Alex's head in his hands as he looked down at several small cuts along her cheek and shoulder. Her white strapless dress had looked beautiful, but had done little to protect her from the glass that had rained down on her. Her left shoulder was spotted with tiny cuts and shards of glass.

Just then, Willard came running out of the back, a large cast iron pan in his hands. "What the..." He looked around.

Grant pulled away and looked around the room. When he saw the large brick that had been tossed through the glass, he bolted from his chair and ran out the front door.

"Grant!" Alex screamed after him.

Taking a few steps onto the sidewalk, he realized the town was completely quiet. It was a quarter past ten on a weeknight and there wasn't a soul out. No cars drove by, he couldn't see anyone running away. Whoever had thrown the brick was long gone.

"Damn it," he said, feeling frustrated he hadn't thought to check outside sooner. He'd been so concerned about Alex.

"Looks like whoever did it is gone." Willard was standing right behind him. When Grant turned around, he nodded. "You okay?" he asked.

"I'm fine. Alex is cut, though." They both made their way back inside where Alex was holding a clean towel over the cut on her shoulder.

Grant had her sit down in a clean booth on the

opposite wall. "Let me take a look." He pulled back the washcloth and looked. The cut on her shoulder was deeper than he'd first thought.

Willard stood over them. "I'll get Jamella to come back down here. Maybe call the sheriff while I'm at it." He turned and walked into the back room.

"You might need stitches." Grant frowned as he gently cleaned the cut.

"There's a first aid kit behind the counter." She pointed towards the cash register. "Just there."

He got up and grabbed the small kit and looked through it. Pulling out the antibiotic cream and gauze, he started cleaning the glass from her skin and hair then dressed some of the larger cuts.

By the time Jamella arrived, he'd dabbled some salve on every tiny cut.

Jamella rushed in the front door. When she saw Alex, she ran over and knelt down. "Are you alright, sweetie?" She took Alex's face in her hands and looked at her. "Oh, my poor child."

"I'm okay, Jamella, really." Alex grabbed Jamella's hand, and Grant could tell that their friendship was stronger than a simple working relationship.

When the sheriff walked in a few seconds later, Jamella started chewing him out.

"Why is it dat someone can do dis"—she flung her arms and motioned in Alex's direction— "and it takes thirty minutes for you to get here?"

"Now, Jamella, calm down." Stephen Miller had been sheriff in Fairplay for as long as anyone could remember. The old man could still move like he was in his thirties, even though his full head of hair was whiter than snow. Everyone in town knew he was still the best shot, since he always took home the blue ribbons for marksmanship at the county fair. It had been rumored once that he'd been married a long time ago, but he hadn't been seen with anyone in a romantic way for a long time.

"I'm sure your insurance will cover the damage," the sheriff said, taking Jamella's shoulders to calm her down.

"I don't give a furry rat's butt 'bout my window, but when dey hurt dis poor child here"—she motioned towards Alex—"dat's when I get mad."

Grant watched with a little humor as he realized how mad Jamella was. The maddest he'd ever seen her, and he'd once witnessed her yelling at an employee for stealing.

"Jamella, I'm okay, really." Alex started to stand up, but Jamella put her hand on her unhurt shoulder.

"You just stay dar, child. Let me handle dis." Then she turned on the sheriff again. "Now, we all knowed who's responsible for dis. The question is…Are you gonna handle dis, or shall I?"

The sheriff's face turned a little red, and Grant

could see understanding and anger come into the old man's eyes.

"Now, Jamella, don't go getting funny ideas in that brain of yours. If there was any proof, if anyone saw Travis do this…" He looked at Grant, who quickly shook his head in frustration. "Then there's nothing I can do. Just because you think it's Travis Nolan, doesn't mean it is." He held up his hand when Jamella started to talk, silencing her. "But I will head that way and ask after his whereabouts in the last hour. Until I have some solid proof, we all know there's nothing I can do to keep that boy behind bars." The sheriff turned and walked out quickly.

"Dat man is useless," Jamella said, crossing her arms over her chest.

"Don't be so hard on him. After all, he's right." Grant sat across from Alex and took her hand in his. "Just because we think it's Travis, doesn't mean it is. It could have been some kids. I've heard there's a group of high school kids that broke into The Rooster liquor store last week. Could be the same kids trying to break in here."

Jamella let out a humpf noise and snatched up the broom and dustpan. "Ain't no kids, we all know dat." She started sweeping up the glass, then she looked at Grant directly. "Take dat girl home and make sure she gets a good night's rest."

He smiled. "Yes ma'am." He got up and reached to help Alex stand.

146

"Don't you need some help?" Alex asked.

"No, child." Jamella walked over and laid a hand gently on Alex's cheek. "You go home with your man now and get some rest." Then she looked at Grant again. "I'm sure I can trust him to make sure you stay safe for the rest of da night."

Grant smiled and nodded. "Yes ma'am."

Jill Sanders

Chapter Ten

"I think Jamella approves of you," Alex said on the ride out of town.

"Yeah?" He glanced over at her. The white bandages on her forehead almost glowed in the darkness.

"Yeah," Alex chuckled. "She always told me Travis was no good and found several ways to keep me at work late when she knew I was going to be out with him."

"Smart woman." Grant smiled.

"Yeah," she said, then sighed. "I guess I should have listened to the people around me more often."

He reached over and took her hand, while steering with his other hand. "What's important is that you've finally come to your senses."

She chuckled. "I suppose you can look at it like

I was temporarily insane."

He chuckled and turned into his driveway, then slammed on his breaks. "Damn it." He jumped out of the truck and walked forward, making sure to keep the headlights on his new corral area.

The damage wasn't that bad, but several of his posts had been pulled out. By the looks of the large ruts in his yard, it had been done by a truck with a winch.

"Oh," Alex said, standing next to him. "How bad is it?" She looked around.

"Not bad," he said as he stood there assessing the damage.

Alex pulled out her cell phone from her purse and dialed the sheriff's number. "Hi, Sheriff, it's Alex. I'm over here at Grant's place and, well, you'd better come over and see for yourself." She paused, then said, "Yeah, we'll be here." When she clicked her phone off, she immediately dialed again.

"Lauren, I'm over at Grant's place." She paused and listened to her sister, and a large smile crossed her face. "Yeah, well, I just wanted you to know what was going on." Alex walked back towards the truck as she filled her sister in on the evening's details.

They were sitting on the front deck when the sheriff pulled in, his lights hitting the downed posts.

"Maybe we caught a break here," he said as he leaned over and looked closer at the tire marks. "If we can tell what type of tires did this damage, then we can compare it to what Travis has on his truck."

Grant felt like a fool for not thinking of it himself. "I've got a spotlight in the back of my truck, if you need more light."

"Sure," the sheriff said, pointing his spotlight in the direction of the tire tracks. When Grant moved closer with his spotlight, the sheriff took out his cell phone and took a few pictures of the tire marks. "I'll check these with Travis' truck first thing in the morning." He shook his head. "Sure made a mess, didn't he?"

"It's only three posts," Grant said, knowing it had taken him almost an hour to place each one.

The sheriff turned to Grant and lowered his voice. "Grant, even if these do match, you know half the men in this county buy tires from one place in town. Hell, I probably have tires that match this on my hunting truck."

"Yeah, still looking for that solid proof." Grant shook his head in disgust.

"Yup." The sheriff tucked his cell phone into his pocket and started walking towards his car. "Well, I'd better get back. 'Night."

Grant watched the sheriff drive back down his driveway, then turned to Alex, who was still sitting on the porch looking very sweet in her dress and boots. Smiling, he walked up the steps and stopped

151

right in front of her.

"Now, where were we before all this mess started?" He pulled her up into his arms and started swaying with her.

She smiled up at him. "What are you doing?"

"Dancing. Before that brick came flying through the window, I was about to ask you to dance." He smiled when she leaned closer and rested her head on his shoulder.

"This is nice." She sighed.

He smiled as he moved around his front porch. "We'll have to hit the Rusty Rail next weekend. The fair will be in town and it's sure to be a great time."

"Oh!" She pulled back, smiling at him. "That sounds great. I can't wait."

He smiled down at her and gently moved a strand of her hair away from her face. "Will you go with me?"

She smiled up at him and nodded. "Of course."

"Will you stay with me tonight?" he asked, holding his breath.

Her smile got bigger and she nodded again. "Yes, of course." She reached up, standing on her toes, and placed a soft kiss on his lips. The sweetness of her kiss undid him. His hands shook as he pulled her hips closer to his. He ran his hands up and over her soft shoulders until he cupped the back of her head, holding her to him. Heat spread so fast throughout, that he almost felt like it was too much, too fast. Then she moaned and he started walking her towards the front door. She laughed when her shoulders came up against the wall next to the door.

"Damn, I'm usually smoother than this." He smiled down at her. "I guess you do something to me."

She looked down his body and smiled. "Yes, I can see what I do to you from here."

He chuckled. "You little witch." He pulled open the screen door and took her hips with his hands and playfully pushed her inside with him. She came to him again, her mouth playing over his as he walked slowly into the house. When the backs of his knees hit the couch, he pulled her down on top of him on the soft cushions. She gasped a little, then settled down on top of him, raining kisses over his jaw and neck. Her hands traveled over his shoulders and arms as she pulled open the buttons on his shirt.

"You looked very nice in this suit. I love what you've done to your body," she said against his skin, trailing kisses across his chest. He leaned back and closed his eyes, enjoying the feel of her mouth on his heated skin.

His hands went to her hips, holding her close to him, but she moved farther down, her fingers going to the snap of his pants.

"Alex," he moaned, "give me a minute." He captured her hands with his. "Come back up here, and let me enjoy you."

She shook her head playfully, then smiled and started to slowly unsnap his pants. He closed his eyes again and tried to mentally slow down. But then her fingers wrapped around him and he moaned her name and begged for more. Her mouth moved over his tight stomach, trailing hot kisses over his perfect six-pack. He reached down and pulled her up, hiking her dress high as his fingers dug into her bare hips. He pulled her to the side as they kissed. Yanking a condom from his pocket, he quickly sheathed himself and pulled her silky panties to the side. When he slid into her heat, she gasped then moaned and sat up a little. She placed her hands on his chest and looked down at him.

"You're the one who wouldn't slow down." He smiled up at her.

"I like the speed," she said, then started moving her hips slowly.

He looked up at her. Her head was tilted back, and her hair lay over her shoulder as she moved above him. Her lips were parted slightly, and he knew that he'd never forget the look of her above him like this. His fingers dug into her hips, holding her down onto him as she moved. Then she leaned over and kissed him, and he felt something shift inside his chest. Her lips were softer, her kisses deeper than he'd ever know, and he could tell nothing would ever be the same again.

154

Alex woke the next morning to rain and thunder and Grant. She smiled over at him as he looked across the pillow at her. "Morning." She yawned and stretched. It was the first time she'd woken up in a bed with a man and she felt just a little uncomfortable.

Without saying anything, he reached over and gently pulled her closer, placing soft kisses on her cheeks and eyes. Her hands came up to touch his chest and desire spread through her like a storm. Rolling over, he pinned her underneath him as his hands started roaming under the covers on her naked skin. This time they made love slowly, taking time to explore each other in the growing daylight. Her hands shook as she lightly ran them over every inch of his body.

Finally, when they came together, she closed her eyes and shut out thoughts about how this meant more to her than any relationship she'd ever had before. She refused to believe that Grant was anything more than a healing step out of a bad relationship.

He made her breakfast as she showered. When she walked into his kitchen, he was standing at the stove cooking and looking damn sexy in just his jeans. Whatever it was, it smelled delicious. Her

155

stomach growled as she sat down at the table. He put a plate in front of her.

"What's this?" She looked down at her plate and frowned a little.

He smiled and sat next to her with his plate. "Turkey bacon and egg white omelets with mushrooms, tomatoes, onions, and green peppers. Trust me." He took up his fork. "I've been eating healthy like this for several years now and I'll never go back." He scooped up a spoonful and moaned when he took a bite.

She had been raised on meat and potatoes. She enjoyed an omelet for breakfast, but usually there was enough bacon and ham in it to stop even the strongest heart. Looking down at her plate, she noticed there was more green stuff in her omelet than meat. Scooping up a small bite, she decided that if it had changed his life so drastically, she'd try it. Especially since he'd turned from the chubby four-eyed kid to the sexy man who sat shirtless in front of her now.

When she tasted the spicy eggs, she fell in love. "Oh, my." She took another bite and another. "These are wonderful!" She looked at him and smiled.

"Told ya." He smiled and took another bite. "You should hit the gym with me sometime." He laughed at the face she made. "Before you say it, no, I don't think you need to lose any weight." He smiled at her. "The gym is quite addictive."

"I don't know. I remember taking gym class in high school. I hated it." She frowned at him, then picked up a piece of her turkey bacon. She'd never tried it before and was desperately wishing for a real piece of bacon. That is, until she bit into it. The meat tasted so good, she thought about stealing a piece off his plate.

"I hated gym class too. Remember Miss Gulden?" he said, frowning.

Alex laughed. "When she wore her red sweatsuit, she looked like a large apple." They laughed.

"As adults, we get to pick and choose what exercises we do. I've found boxing is what I like best. You'd be good at it." His smile turned mischievous. "It'll give you another option rather than kicking a man where it counts."

She chuckled. "I suppose I could add some new tools to my vast arsenal of weapons." She held up her arms and flexed her biceps as he laughed.

By the time Grant drove her home, she had decided to spend the rest of her day in Tyler. She was going to search for the right phone for him and possibly pick up a few items for herself while she was at it.

Haley decided to go along with her. She was thankful for the company and the help in picking out a few other items. Their first stop was to a baby store where they spent several hours picking out items for Lauren and Chase. When they walked next door to the phone store, the two of them were having so much fun laughing about what they'd bought their sister that they didn't realize that Savannah was standing right in front of them. She was standing on the sidewalk, a cigarette hanging from her lips, and they almost plowed her right over.

"Oh!" Haley said, backing up a few steps. Alex held the packages from the baby store in one hand and made sure to put her sister behind her.

"Well, well, well," Savannah purred, puffing smoke in their direction. "What do we have here?" she said in a sarcastic tone, her eyes darting between them.

"None of your business." Haley coughed, and jutted out her chin, glaring at the other woman.

Alex found it humorous how her sister treated Savannah, considering she'd broken up Alex's relationship, not Haley's. She felt even more love for her little sister, knowing Haley would gladly hold Savannah down while Alex pummeled her. She was over Travis. She was over Savannah. And more important, she was over having them punish her for something that wasn't her fault.

Handing Haley her bags, Alex stepped closer to Savannah and watched the other woman's eyes heat. "You know what I'm tired of, Haley?"

She glared at the woman as her sister chuckled behind her and answered, "No, what?"

Savannah put out her cigarette with her heel and

158

looked back at her with a smirk.

"I'm tired of being treated like the bad person in this whole fiasco. I'm tired of people taking it out on someone who had nothing to do with two people cheating on another innocent person. I'm tired of having Grant's tires slashed." She watched Savannah's face, but her eyes showed nothing, no hint of guilt or knowledge. "I'm tired of having his property destroyed. And," she stepped forward until she was only a breath away, "I'm tired of having people throw things at me." She watched as a smile slowly crept onto Savannah's lips. "Now, if we're done with this"–she paused and looked Savannah up and down—"I want nothing more than to move on with my life." She turned around and reached for her bags, then walked away without another word.

"That bitch," Haley said under her breath.

"Don't." Alex stopped her just inside the cell phone place. "Don't give her another thought. We all knew what she was before that night with Travis, and we all know it won't be the last time. I only wish those two would get married." She looked out the front windows and watched Savannah head across the parking lot alone. "They deserve each other. But," she sighed, "sadly, I've heard that they aren't even officially seeing each other."

Haley looked out the window, following Alex's gaze. "She's an attention seeker. She'll do anything — and anyone—to get attention."

Alex turned to her sister and smiled. "So, let's not give it to her. I've got a cell phone to buy." She smiled. "We're hitting the frozen yogurt place afterwards."

"Woohoo." Haley smiled and did a fist pump.

Chapter Eleven

Grant spent the rest of his day cleaning up the mess that was his corral. It didn't take him long to drop the timbers back into the holes they'd been torn out of. He made sure to compact the dirt around them again so they were just as strong as the first time. Some of the cross timbers were beyond repair, and he needed to head to the lumberyard first thing in the morning to replace them.

Just before sunset, he walked into his barn and checked up on his animals. The three Powerpuff sisters were doing well. They'd mastered escaping their pen so that they always ended up loose in the barn at night. He spent a few minutes playing with the animals after feeding them. He really enjoyed each and every one and thought of them as family.

When he walked back to the house, his mind

wandered to last night and having Alex in his bed. He was just opening his door when he heard a car drive up. His heart skipped when he noticed Alex's car parking behind his truck. How is it that just the sight of her made him feel like a schoolboy with a crush?

Smiling, he walked to the edge of the porch as she walked up the steps.

"Evening," he said as she walked right into his arms.

"Hi." She went up on her toes and kissed his lips. The feel and smell of her had his head almost spinning. "I have something for you." She smiled and his mind flashed to images of her in nothing but a red bow and heels. His smile fell away a little when she held up a small yellow bag with a bow on top.

"What's this?" He walked her over to the bench underneath the living room window and sat next to her.

She handed him the bag and smiled. "Well, I was doing some thinking the other day about your new business with your father." She smiled and, not waiting for him to open the bag, reached over and pulled it open, handing him a small box. "I hope you don't mind." She looked up at him, waiting for his eyes to show the emotion she'd hoped would flash there. "I know it's your birthday in a week."

He looked down at the box and to be honest, it

took him a few seconds for it to register. It had been a few years since he'd purchased anything like it. Slowly, he let a smile creep to his face

"Seriously?" He looked down at the box and thought of a million things he wanted to do with the new toy in his hands.

"Yeah." Her voice didn't sound as sure as it had a second ago. He looked up at her and saw the uncertainty in her dark eyes.

Setting the box on his lap, he took her face into his hands and kissed her, showing her what he was feeling. A few minutes and a million heartbeats later, he pulled away, a little breathless. "It's perfect. Of course"—he looked down at her gift and then back up at her—"you're going to have to show me how to use it."

She smiled. "That's the plan."

Two hours and a few hundred apps later, the new Android phone sat on the coffee table, forgotten. Since the evening had cooled off to the low fifties, he lit a fire in the stone fireplace that sat along his living room wall. They huddled together, not for warmth, but for need. He didn't feel like he could get close enough to her. There were too many clothes and his fingers just wouldn't cooperate as they roamed over her delicate skin.

When their clothes hit the floor, they slowly moved together, their breaths matching in the fading light. The light of the fire behind her lit up her hair so it looked like she wore a halo. Her face was in shadows, but the light accented her curves and he couldn't stop himself from running his hands up and down her sides, enjoying her softness. She leaned forward and when her sexy scent hit him, and her soft skin rubbed up against his face and chest, he couldn't hold himself back any longer. Using his hands on her hips, he easily reversed their positions until he was kneeling at the edge of the couch, her legs wrapped around him as her hair fanned out on the cushions.

The dim firelight cast a warm glow over her skin, making her look even softer, somehow.

"Grant?" Alex looked up at him in question. He hadn't realized he'd stopped moving until she spoke, her voice a sexy whisper in the quiet room. He'd been looking at her, just looking. She was more beautiful than...well, than anyone he'd ever known. All he knew was that his chest felt tight when he looked at her, his heart skipped several beats, and his knees went weak.

He began moving again, this time leaning down to her and taking that sweet mouth with his until he felt her follow him in surrender.

When he felt her body relax, he pulled her down with him to the soft rug in front of the fireplace. Pulling a blanket and some couch pillows with him, he positioned them so she lay in front of him, looking into the fire.

"This is nice." She sighed and rubbed his arm

with her fingertips.

"Yes." He smiled into her hair. "I'm enjoying myself, as well." She chuckled.

"You know…" She stopped her fingers over his elbow and twisted around until she looked at him. "I'm entered in the barrel races next week." She turned back around.

He smiled. "You've won the blue ribbon every year that I can remember. You'll do great."

"Oh, I know I will." She chuckled. "I was just thinking that you should try steer wrestling or at least enter Mojo and the girls into the dairy goat competition. I think the girls will be old enough by then."

He chuckled. "I'd thought about it myself. I'm pretty proud of them all, but Buttercup is going to win the blue ribbon."

"Really?" She turned and smiled at him. "Have a soft spot for the rough girls, huh?"

"You know it." He smiled and pulled her hair playfully.

It was after midnight when they finally made it into the bedroom. He carried her while she tried to distract him, and he almost dropped her on her beautifully naked rear end several times. She laughed and held on, trying to make him cross-eyed using her mouth and hands.

When his alarm went off at four the next morning, she moaned and covered her head with the pillow.

"Early hours for a farmer and a lawyer." He'd quickly shut it off and apologized. She'd rolled over and moaned again as he laughed. "You stay there, don't move." He kissed her exposed neck and heard a different kind of moan. He moved to get out of bed, but she rolled over and pulled him back to her.

The animals complained when he walked into the barn almost an hour late. He was greeted by the Powerpuff girls, and they showed their disapproval of his tardiness by continuously butting his leg with their heads.

"Okay, okay. Hold your horses. You know," he talked to them as he poured their feed, "you'll understand one day. Won't they, Mojo?" He smiled when the mother goat bleated at him in understanding. "But for now, enjoy your food." He moved on to the horses and talked to each as he went, thinking of Alex and the rodeo.

The West sisters had always played a large part in the county rodeo. First and foremost was their cattle. They always had the blue ribbon steer and heifer, not to mention Alex's talent during barrel racing. Haley had entered several other animals, all of which, he had no doubt, had placed as well.

When he was younger, he'd tried mutton busting, but after almost breaking his glasses, his mother had forbid him to get near anything wild like that again. He'd always wanted to try his hand at calf roping or steer wrestling, like Alex had suggested. He had done it before, just never as a competition. Maybe he'd swing by the fairgrounds and see what it took to enter.

When he went back in the house an hour later, he walked in to wonderful, warm smells. He'd left Alex in his bed and had thought she'd stay put, but she was standing behind the stove, his apron over shorts and a cream-colored blouse. Her hair was braided in two braids and covered with a red bandana. When she turned and smiled at him, a spatula in her hands, he forgot to breathe.

"I thought I'd make us some breakfast. But since all you have is health food, I decided to make pancakes." She chuckled.

"You didn't have to cook." He walked over and wrapped his arms around her, pulling her back up against his front as she flipped a pancake. "Smells wonderful," he said as he buried his face into her hair.

"Me or the food?" She giggled.

"Both." He kissed her shoulder. "How about some coffee?"

"Sounds good. I have a cup there." She nodded towards an empty mug. He walked over and filled one for himself and refilled hers, then went to work setting the table.

Over breakfast they talked about the rodeo, his website, and his plans for the farm. When his new phone rang, he answered and was surprised to hear

167

his father on the other side.

"So, you're finally getting with the times, huh, boy?" his father joked. He could hear his mother talking in the background, then his father told her, "I'm getting to it. Give me a chance to tell the boy hi, first." Then his father said to him. "We just wanted to ask if you're coming to dinner this Friday."

"Friday?" He looked over at Alex and smiled, knowing what was coming next. When she smiled and nodded, he said, "Sure. Is it okay if I bring a guest?"

His father laughed and he could just imagine his mom dancing in the background. "Sure, Alexis is always welcome here. We'll see you around seven."

He hung up with his dad and reached over and took Alex's hand. "You've just made my parents very happy."

She smiled back at him. "I like your folks. Did you know that they meet at the diner every Monday for lunch together? They are so cute. They hold hands and sit side by side." She sighed, then looked down at their joined hands.

"Yeah," he chuckled. "But I try not to think of my parents as cute."

How dare they? Did they not understand the signs? Couldn't they see what was plain in front of them? Everyone in town knew they didn't belong together. But they kept on seeing each other. Now, she was staying at his place!

Hands banged against the steering wheel in frustration. This was too much!

A plan slowly formed as the car pulled away. Think! When would there be another opportunity to strike?

Then the fog of anger cleared and peace settled. The rodeo was coming up. What a perfect time. But this time it needed to be something bigger. Something well thought out and planned. There was a lot to do before and little time to execute it all.

Yes, this would be the final move in this wild, fun game.

Alex pulled the reins tighter and felt the rush of being pulled in the opposite direction as she rounded the barrel quickly. She dug her heels into Sophie's sides, sending the horse rushing towards the next barrel. She'd practiced with the horse almost every day for the past year; this was her sport. She smiled when she pulled to a stop just through the gate. She looked over at Chase just as he nodded and smiled.

"Beat your last time by three seconds." He removed his hat and wiped at the sweat rolling down his brow. The nights might be cooling off, but the days were still hot and sultry. Sweat was rolling down Alex's back and she itched for a cold shower, but she wanted to beat even her latest time. When it came to racing, Alex demanded to be the fastest.

Letting Sophie rest for a few minutes, she jumped down and took a drink from the water bottle Chase offered her. She smiled over at him. "You know, I was thinking about moving back into my old room, so that you two can have the larger one for the baby." She leaned against the post and watched Sophie. "Lauren would like the baby to grow up in her old room." She turned and looked at Chase. When she noticed that he was frowning, she stood up and asked, "What?"

He looked up at her, then shook his head. "Oh, no, it's nothing. I was just thinking of everything that still needs to be done to the house before the baby comes along. There's baby-proofing the entire place. Not to mention painting. I think some of the walls still have lead paint on them." He frowned some more as Alex laughed. It was his turn to ask, "What?"

"You." Alex said, smiling at her brother-in-law.

"Did you ever think you'd be talking about what kind of paint you needed for your baby's room?" She looked at him, really looked at him. He was tall like Grant. But where Chase had almost jet-black hair and dark chocolate eyes, Grant's soft, curly, sandy hair made his light blue eyes shine. The men were almost equally matched in form, but for some reason Grant filled out his shirts better. Maybe she was biased?

"Hey." She leaned back again and smiled. "I've got another idea. It'll be tricky pulling it off, but I think with everyone's help, we can surprise Lauren." She smiled, planning everything out in her head.

"What do you have in mind?" Chase asked, looking a little worried.

She laughed. "Come on." She grabbed his arms and started pulling him towards the barn where she was certain Haley would be, brushing Oliver, her two-year-old steer. "I'll tell you and Haley together." She pulled him into the cool barn, found Haley, and proceeded to tell them her plans to surprise Lauren. She'd watched a show where a group of people had remodeled a room in one day while the expectant mother was out. When she came home, the baby's room was completed. She thought that if they got enough people together, and could keep Haley from blurting it out, that they could surprise Lauren that way. When they walked out of the barn half an hour later, everyone had tasks they needed to complete for the event to happen. First things first—Alex had to move out of the bigger room.

That evening, Grant picked her up at a quarter past eight, and they headed to the Rusty Rail for karaoke night. Everyone in town always ended up at the bar one Thursday night out of every month. Even Chase and Lauren were going to be there. Haley had called off going that night, due to a headache.

When Grant drove up, the small parking lot was full, so they pulled into the field across the train tracks and parked next to Lauren's truck.

"It's packed tonight," Alex said, looking at the lights coming from the old building. Loud music could be heard whenever someone opened the door. The wood building had been remodeled after the big tornado that had swept through eighteen years ago, the one that had taken Alex's mother.

Under the new green metal roof, the town of Fairplay had seen more than its fair share of action in the form of fights, though most fights here were between close friends or family members and almost always ended up over a cold beer.

As they walked towards the door, hand in hand, Alex felt a little nervous. This was their first time out in public as a couple. Since the breakup, she'd learned what people had thought about her relationship with Travis. Most people had smiled and told her how sweet they were together when they were engaged, but after their breakup, everyone proceeded to tell her that Travis was no good and not right for her. Would people do the same to her and Grant?

She looked over at Grant and noticed his eyes were glued to the door. His profile was something to dream about. His nose was perfect. His jaw was strong and sexy and he had just the right amount of stubble over his face. His blue dress shirt and old, worn-in jeans looked even sexier since they fit like a glove. His black hat caused shadows to fall over his face, sheltering his eyes. He looked like a sexy, dangerous cowboy who knew what he wanted and how to get it.

But it was more than his appearance that had her holding onto his hand and smiling up at him. He was the kindest person she knew, besides her brother-in-law. Grant treated her like she was something special. She'd never been treated like that by a boyfriend before. She looked at him more closely; he looked as nervous as she felt. Pulling on his hand, she stopped him at the base of the stairs and wrapped her arms around his shoulders. His nervous smile almost stopped her heart. What was she doing with someone so pure?

"Have I told you how beautiful you look tonight?" He whispered it to her, pulling her up a little more until they were looking eye to eye.

She shook her head, not trusting her voice since her throat had gone dry.

"You look amazing," he said as his hands

rubbed up and down her sides and arms. "I'm the luckiest man here." She'd worn one of her favorite jean skirts and a black lacy top that buttoned up the front and showed off her hot pink tank top. Her matching earrings and jewelry accented the pink glow of her skin. His eyes traveled over her, resting on her lips.

She wrapped her fingers around his neck, pulling him down until their lips met. The zing she felt when his lips touched hers went straight to her toes, causing them to curl in her boots. When she finally pulled back, she was breathless and her eyesight was a little misty.

He rested his forehead on hers and smiled. "Are you sure you want to go in?"

She laughed and nodded her head, just as the door opened and loud music came pumping out, making her want to dance. Grabbing his hand, her confidence boosted, she rushed through the door, a large smile on her lips as they glided through the full room, straight to the dance floor.

His arms wrapped around her, pulling her close as they moved across the old wood dance floor. Spinning along with other couples, they swayed with the music, smiling and laughing together. Grant had a talent for dancing. He spun her, lifted her, and dipped her, and did it all very smoothly. She'd never danced with anyone as smooth as him before. When the song was over, they walked over to the table where Chase and Lauren sat. Chase was nursing a beer, Lauren sipping what looked like Sprite and cranberry juice.

"Evening." Grant nodded to them.

"You two look good out there." Chase smiled and nodded to the waitress, lifting his fingers to signal they needed two more beers.

"Where did you learn to dance like that?" She sat on the chair, breathless.

He smiled. "My mother would never let me go to any school dances, but that didn't stop her from teaching me all the moves."

Alex remembered that Grant's mother was a god-fearing woman, highly involved with all the church events. She was even the secretary at the local Baptist Church.

"Smooth," Lauren said, taking another small sip of her drink. Alex noticed that she looked a little pale.

Leaning over, she whispered to her sister, "Are you feeling okay?"

Lauren nodded a little and closed her eyes. When she ran from the table towards the bathroom, Alex apologized and followed her sister.

She rushed into the bathroom, just in time to hear her sister lose her dinner. She didn't know what to do, so she stood outside the door, wishing she could do something, anything to help her.

When Lauren walked out of the stall, a hand on her stomach and a smile on her face, Alex encased her in a hug.

"Are you okay? Maybe we should take you home?" She pulled back and looked at her sister. Her eyes were a little dull. Her skin color was coming back, but she could see she wasn't back to her normal self, yet.

Lauren shook her head, "No, I'll be fine now." She walked over and rinsed her mouth out, looking in the mirror at her sister. "I almost always only throw up once. Now it'll settle down." She put a hand over her stomach again.

Alex wrapped her arms around her sister. "I'll be glad when the morning sickness is over."

They both heard a squeal and looked over to see Savannah's back receding out the bathroom door.

Lauren looked over and shrugged. "Now at least we know that the news will travel fast." She chuckled. "Come on, I'm sure my husband is worried sick."

They walked out and when Chase saw them, he rushed over and took his wife in a light hug, whispering to her. Alex walked over and sat next to Grant, smiling to him. "She's okay." She picked up her cold beer and took a sip as the couple came back and sat down.

"Alex, tell your sister we should head home." Chase frowned and motioned towards Lauren.

Alex shook her head. "If you can get her to do something she doesn't want to, then you have more

176

influence over her than I've ever had."

Lauren laughed. "I'm fine, really." She took a sip of her drink and smiled. "Besides, you promised to dance with me, cowboy." She pulled Chase up off the chair and walked with him to the dance floor. Alex sighed when she saw them slowly gliding across the floor in each other's arms.

"They look good together," Grant said next to her ear. His arm came around her shoulders, pulling her closer.

"Yeah," she sighed again, "they do."

Just then Savannah walked up to them with two of her friends, a sneer plastered on her face.

"I hear congratulations are in order." She crossed her arms over her chest, causing the buttons on the front of her red blouse to almost pop.

Alex nodded, not really giving her any attention. She knew she was just trying to provoke her in front of her friends. So instead, she pulled Grant away towards the dance floor.

"What was that all about?" he whispered into her ear as they slowly moved to the sad song.

"She walked into the bathroom right after Lauren was sick. She's been a friend of Lauren's since they were kids. The least I can do is be polite when it concerns Lauren." She leaned back and smiled up at him. "Doesn't mean I have to actually talk to her, though."

He chuckled. "You know, I never did like that girl. She used to call me hippo." He frowned and she could see the pain in his eyes. "Hungry hippo."

"How horrible." Alex looked around for Savannah, feeling like dumping something over her head again. Maybe a pitcher of beer?

He chuckled. "I'm supposed to be the one defending your honor, not the other way around."

"Hmm. What?" She looked back up at him.

He chuckled and shook his head. "Never mind. Forget her. It was a long time ago and it didn't mean anything." He leaned in and kissed her softly on the lips. "Besides, it made me a stronger person." He kissed her again as they swayed on the dance floor.

"Mmmm, what were we talking about?" She laughed and pulled him down for another kiss.

Chapter Twelve

That night Alex stayed at Grant's place again. He loved that he woke with her sexy scent filling his senses. Her soft skin was up against his, and when he opened his eyes and looked at her sleeping face, he started dreaming of their future together.

Tonight was the dinner with his folks, and even though he was a little nervous to bring her over, he was very eager to make it official with his folks. It wasn't as if they didn't know Alex. His dad and her dad had been best friends since grade school. He even thought that his folks were godparents to all three of the West sisters, but he wasn't sure.

He rolled over slightly and watched her sleep for the last few minutes before the alarm went off. Her blonde hair was tied back in a loose braid, which fell over her shoulder. It was soft and smelled of flowers. She'd brought some stuff over and now his bathroom was slowly filling up with sexy smelling bottles.

Her skin was soft and the color of ripe peaches. Her lips were pink and always tasted so good that he never wanted to stop tasting them. Reaching over, he ran his fingertips over her cheek. In sleep, she moaned and snuggled closer to him, causing his body to react to the nearness of her naked one. Closing his eyes, he thought that if she woke, he might be late feeding the livestock again. When her dark eyes slid open, he knew he wouldn't be leaving the bed for a while.

When he finally made it outside, he walked out onto the porch to rain and thunder. He went back in and grabbed his rain jacket and boots and made his morning rounds.

By noon the sun had broken through the layer of clouds, and sweat was pouring down his back as he worked with one of his new horses. Alex had left shortly after sun up, heading into work at the diner. He was going to pick her up at home around six thirty so they would be at his folks in plenty of time for dinner. His mother was a stickler for punctuality. She always had been, so he'd learned at an early age to be someone who was always early.

He'd gotten the corral back up and the smaller animals spent a lot of time there playing in the sun, while the horses and cattle spent their days in the larger fields.

He loved that his little piece of land was crowded with all kinds of animals. He'd never really been allowed a pet growing up, though he'd tried several times as a child to talk his parents into it. His mother was the classic Type A personality and vacuumed and swept at least four times a day. Animal hair was the last thing she would have allowed in her house.

Over the years, he'd brought home everything from kittens to a small alligator he'd found in the grass behind a dumpster when they'd taken a trip near the coast one weekend.

He'd begged his mother to let him keep the little guy when she'd caught him letting Roger swim in the bathtub. It had been three days since he'd snuck him into the house under his jacket. He'd promised her that Roger would live in the bathtub and wouldn't get the rest of the house dirty. But in the end, his father had taken Roger away, promising he'd deliver him back to the water.

As he looked around his yard now, he smiled at the diversity he saw there. He had a lot of different kinds of animals, but no alligators.

He chuckled at the geese and ducks as they fought for space in his small pond. For some reason they kept coming back, and even though he technically had no claim to them, he thought of them as his. It didn't hurt that he threw them his stale bread every day. He knew they nested in the tall grass around the smaller pond.

181

He smiled and looked around again. The place was his, and there was no way he was going to leave it anytime soon. It was home, and he knew who he wanted to share it with in the future.

He looked off towards the house where he could just imagine Alex coming out the back door and waving at him. Children would be running around the trimmed back yard, chasing each other, three of them, maybe four. She'd plant flowers in all the window boxes and along the back pathway; their sunny faces would catch the sunlight.

Looking down at his watch, he realized he'd spent too much time daydreaming and was likely going to be late. Gathering the animals, he tucked them away for the night and went in to shower and change, making sure to put on his good shirt and tie for his mother's sake.

When he drove through Saddleback Ranch's gates, he noticed the large herd of cattle being driven into the fields by half-a-dozen ranch hands. Waving, he continued up the long drive and stopped in front of the front porch. The place was sure big, almost triple the size of his house.

He knew the third floor was a large attic, but even so, the place had enough room for the four people living in it to be comfortable. His heart skipped and he began wondering what it would take to convince Alex to live in a smaller place.

By the time he walked up to the front door and knocked, he'd pretty much talked himself into

182

believing that she'd never agree to live on a small farm with a man who used to be chubby and nearsighted and the victim of bullying.

As the door opened, he wondered why she was even agreeing to go to dinner with him at all. Nothing could have prepared him for the classy woman he saw on the other side of the threshold.

Alex was so nervous, she'd changed her outfit seven times. A new record. She finally ran into Haley's room wrapped in only her towel and started digging through her closet. When Haley walked in ten minutes later, she squealed.

"What are you doing?" Haley bent down and picked up the brown skirt Alex had tossed on the floor by accident.

"Help!" She turned around with a desperate look in her eyes. "Dinner. The Holton's. Less than an hour away."

Haley smiled and grabbed her sister's shoulders. "Breathe. We'll make it through this." Then she closed her eyes and Alex could tell she was imagining the best outfit. Alex knew that Haley had a talent for seeing which clothes would be perfect, so she stood silent until finally Haley opened her eyes and a large smile crossed her face.

"Come with me." She tugged her hand until she followed her down the hall. At first Alex thought she meant to take her into Lauren and Chase's room. Lauren had nice clothes, but she was at least two sizes bigger around the hips than Alex. Even Haley's clothes were a whole size bigger, but with the right belt, Alex could have made it happen. But when Haley walked past her sister's bedroom, she felt even more frustrated.

"Where are you taking me?" She tugged a little on her sister's hand.

"Wait and see." Haley pulled her towards the door that lead up to the attic. Alex hadn't been up there in years. To be honest, she didn't want to go up there. There were too many memories of her mother, too many emotions. She'd avoided opening the heavy wood door as long as she could. Now she followed Haley up the narrow stairs, listening to them creak as they made their way into the darkness above.

"Haley." She felt like pulling away from her sister's light grip and running.

"Just wait. You're going to love this. I was up here the other day, seeing if there was anything up here for our surprise." She whispered the last part. "Anyway, I stumbled upon this old trunk full of clothes. I think they were Grandma's, maybe Mother's." She shrugged her shoulder and dropped Alex's hand. "Anyway, I found the most perfect dress." Haley bent down and opened the lid of the old box.

Alex's first thought was that anything that came from it must be too old and destroyed by now, but when Haley fished around and pulled out a square of dark gray material, Alex took a step closer.

"What is that?" She bent down and took the square from her sister. Haley sat back and smiled.

Alex opened the vacuum-sealed bag and pulled out the dress. It was gorgeous. The light material easily straightened as she shook it out. A large collar crossed over the breasts and hung below the shoulders on the sides; the half-sleeves would hit her mid-arm. There were two oversized buttons that would sit across her lower ribs, just above a wide black belt with a simple silver buckle. The skirt flared out, and when she held it up to her, she realized it would hit her mid-calf.

Looking down at Haley, she smiled. "It's perfect."

"Oh…" Haley turned and dug around the trunk again. "There are shoes." She pulled out pair after pair, some of which Alex swore she'd come back upstairs and try on later. Finally, she pulled out a pair of simple yet elegant black heels, which would have been all the rage in the thirties. If only they fit.

Haley set them down in front of her, since her feet were bare. She slipped right into them and closed her eyes at the comfort she found.

"If they were a size smaller, Lauren would fit into them, or a size bigger and they'd be perfect for me. But," Haley looked up at Alex and smiled, "they were meant for you. They're perfect."

She smiled down at her little sister and for a moment believed in destiny. It took almost a half an hour for her to settle on a hairstyle. In the end, she let Lauren come in and tie her hair up in a bun at the top of her head. Lauren had rushed back to her room and pulled out their mother's pearl earrings and choker to finish the ensemble. Looking in the full-length mirror in Lauren's room, the three sisters sighed together.

"You look like mother," Lauren said, under her breath.

"Really?" Alex turned a little, and the skirt of the dress twirled around her. She could barely remember what her mother had looked like. But she had to admit, she'd never looked better. None of her short skirts and tube tops had ever done what the simple, elegant dress was doing for her now. Classy was the best word for it. Now if she could just pull it off for the night, maybe she wouldn't screw up her relationship with Grant.

Five minutes before he was scheduled to arrive, she put the finishing touches on her make up and walked down the stairs to wait. Haley had snapped a few pictures of her as she'd walked down the long staircase. Her sister had always tried to capture special moments such as this, but for the most part, she and Lauren had done everything they could to avoid posing for long sessions in front of their sister's camera.

"Just one more," Haley said just as the light knock sounded at the door.

Alex walked over and, taking a deep breath, pulled open the door.

The look on Grant's face was priceless. He was only jolted out of his shocked state by the click of Haley's camera. His eyes blinked a few times, and she thought she saw him sway a little.

Reaching out, she took his arm and laughed. "Grant?" He looked good in a black blazer and slacks. His collared shirt was loose at the top, and he'd left the top button undone.

"Just give me a moment." He closed his eyes quickly, then re-opened them. A smile slowly crossed his lips. "Wow."

Alex smiled and Lauren and Haley laughed in the background.

"Wow," he said again and shook his head slightly. "Where—?" He started, then shook his head again.

"It was our grandmother's. Well, at least we think it was. Do you like it?" She turned for him, showing him how the skirt swayed with her movements.

"I love it. You look so..." He shook his head again as she smiled.

"Thank you." Then she looked down and smiled even more. "Are those for me?"

"Huh?" He looked down at the small bouquet of white flowers he was carrying. They looked as soft as the material she was wearing and no doubt smelled as good. "Oh, yeah." He handed them to her, his eyes still fixed on her. Then his eyes traveled down to her feet and she saw him struggling all over again.

"Lauren, would you put these in some water. I'm sure Grant would like to get to his parents' place before they start serving dessert." She chuckled as Lauren stepped forward and took the flowers from her, but not before she buried her face in and drank in their sweet scent.

When she turned, he held out his elbow for her to take. She placed her hand through his and held onto him as they walked to the edge of the porch.

"Hey!" Haley said, and when they turned around, she snapped a picture of them together. "Thanks! Have a wonderful night." Then her sister shut the door as they laughed.

By the time they drove up to his parents' house, she'd talked herself into being nervous again. She didn't know why. After all, she'd seen his parents every week of her life. She knew every detail about them and had on numerous occasions been over to their house. But this time, it was different. She still couldn't put her finger on why, other than she wanted their approval for seeing their son. It wasn't as if she was going to marry him. After the whole ordeal with Travis, she'd sworn off marrying anyone for at least several years. After all, twenty-four was way too young to know what you wanted, or who you wanted to be with, for the rest of your life.

Grant walked right in the front door without knocking. The place was just as she remembered it —spotless. Her house was clean, but nothing compared to this. Not even Grant's house was kept this clean. Alex was sure that a crew from Better Homes and Gardens was waiting just outside to rush in and take pictures of the place for the next month's magazine. There were fresh flowers on the tables in crystal vases, and little doilies sat on the shiny wood surfaces to keep the vases from damaging them. The old wood floors gleamed, and she swore she could see her reflection in them.

Just then Grant's father walked into the front room. "Oh, there you are." His dad smiled and crossed the sitting room, shaking Grant's hand.

"I brought beer." Grant held up the six-pack and shook it.

"That's a good boy." His father took the case from him and reached for Alex's hand. "Alexis, you're looking very lovely tonight." He smiled and leaned down and kissed the back of her hand. "A spitting image of Laura."

She hadn't heard her mother's name in years. It still shocked her to hear people talk about her, especially when they had a sad look in their eyes upon mentioning her.

"Glenn?" Grant's mother Carolyn came walking

into the room. Her simple flowered skirt and silver top looked pristine, as did her husband's shirt and slacks. "Oh, there you are. Right on time, too." His mother smiled and walked—no, more like glided —over to them, and placed a kiss on her son's cheek. She turned to Alex and her smile got bigger. "Oh, look at you." She took Alex's hands and held them out. "How beautiful." She looked her up and down with a smile on her face. "What a lovely dress, it suits you well." She leaned in and placed a kiss on her cheek as well.

"Thank you, Mr. and Mrs. Holton. Thank you both for having me tonight," Alex said nervously.

Grant's father huffed. "What's all this Mr. and Mrs. stuff? You've been calling us by our first names since you could talk. No use in changing that now." His father walked over and took her hand from his wife's. "Now, tell me all about how you plan on beating everyone in the barrel races tomorrow." He walked her into the back of the house, towards the dining room.

By the time the chocolate mousse was served, Alex was sure she'd have to loosen the belt around her waist. She hadn't eaten such a wonderful homemade dinner in years. Although Travis' parents prided themselves on being some of the best hosts in town, she'd never warranted a dinner invitation. Not even after their engagement had been announced. She'd never even really been inside their large mansion, which sat at the top of a hill, just inside the town's city limits.

190

Grant's folks, Glenn and Carol, as they had always liked to be called, had been old family friends. Her mother had been best friends with Carol all throughout high school.

"Carol, do I really look like my mother?" she asked her as they sat out on their back porch under the candles and tea lights as the men stoked the fire in the fire pit and drank beer.

Carol looked at her and sighed. "Yes, dear. Out of you three girls, you are the one that reminds me the most of Laura. Not only do you have her eyes, I hear you have her singing voice." She smiled and leaned over to pat her hand.

Alex nodded her head. "Dad used to tell me that." She looked down at her hands sadly. "I wish I could remember more about her."

"Oh…" Carol stood up quickly. "I can help you out, there. I don't know why I've never thought about it before." She turned to her husband and said. "Glenn, why don't you grab the old projector from the garage. Grant, follow him and bring the old movie screen. We'll sit out here for a treat."

As the men walked off towards the garage, Alex watched Carol rush into the house. "You stay right there," she said over her shoulder with a grin. "You're going to love this."

Ten minutes later, after listening to Grant's father explain to him how to open the old movie screen, they all sat in the cushioned porch chairs as the old projector flicked on.

191

Black-and-white images of teenagers on the old high school stage filled the screen. The noise coming from the projectors speaker was garbled. The high school auditorium looked the same. Even the same dark curtain hung in the background.

"I think your mother was up next," Carol said, fast-forwarding the old film. "Here we go." She walked back over and sat down next to her husband.

Then Alex saw her mother step up on stage with an old guitar. She wore a white skirt and a light-colored blouse. Her hair was a little longer than Alex's and hung much like hers did, straight with the slightest of wave. Then she started to play and Alex forgot to breathe. She listened to her mother belt out an old Dolly Parton song, her voice soft and much like Alex's as she sang:

Sometimes I try to count the ways and reasons that I love you
But I can never seem to count that far
I love you in a million ways and for a million reasons
But more than this I love you as you are
More than this I love you just as you are

You are my inspiration, you are the song I sing
You are what makes me happy, you are my everything
You are my daily sunshine, you are my ev'ning star
Ev'rything I'd ever hoped to find, that's what you are
Ev'rything I'll ever want for 'mine', is what you are

As the song progressed, she felt tears slipping

down her cheeks. Grant slipped his hand in hers as her eyes focused, unblinking on the woman who had given up her life for theirs.

She could faintly remember her mother whispering to her before bed, leaning down and placing a soft kiss on her forehead, saying to her, "You are my everything."

When the song ended, the audience at the gym stood and applauded.

Carol handed her a tissue and she quietly wiped her face.

"Thank you." She smiled at her mother's best friend and knew that she had a new memory of her mother that she would never forget.

Chapter Thirteen

Grant dropped Alex off shortly before ten. She had a big day tomorrow, which he knew would start before the crack of dawn. He'd entered Mojo and the girls into the fair and had to be there early, as well. They would be competing against thirty other goats for the blue ribbon, so the competition was stiff. The girls had to be loaded up and delivered to their stalls no later than seven tomorrow morning.

They had decided Alex had better stay home that night since she had to load up and be there herself shortly before then.

He tossed and turned for the first hour, then finally gave up and text her.

"You awake?"

She replied a few seconds later. "Yes."

195

"I miss you. What would you say if I climbed up your drain pipe and crawled in your window?"

"I'd say it's a good thing Chase reinforced our gutters last spring. LOL."

"?"

"LOL? It means laugh out loud."

"Oh, I'm still learning how to do all this. How are you typing so fast?"

"LOL, do you see the little microphone button on the bottom left? Click it, then speak clearly into your phone and hit send."

He tried it and watched as what he'd said showed up on the screen automatically.

"What does this...Oh, how cool is this?"

He tried saying a few other things, getting used to the new technology. Finally, he text, *"Well, I better let you go. Good luck tomorrow."*

"Thanks, you too. I'll see you around. I'll try to stop by the girls' barn before I'm on. Miss you."

"Miss you too, night."

He lay there for a while longer, thinking of Alex before finally drifting off.

Morning came too quickly and things didn't go smoothly. By the time Grant had the girls loaded up, he'd had to change into his back-up shirt. All of them except Buttercup had walked easily into the trailer. Buttercup, however, had decided it was time to play in the mud that had formed from the rain two nights earlier. After hosing her off and trying to dry her the best he could, he'd rushed into the house and changed. He got to the rodeo grounds on time, but then had to sit and wait in all the mess as everyone unloaded their animals. It took almost two hours, with the help of several fairground hands, to unload the girls and get them tucked into their spots. He'd been given numbers for each one that matched the numbers that hung on their gates. He took a few minutes to brush each one and make sure they were clean, especially Buttercup.

When he finally wandered away from the large barn, he headed towards the food booths. The sky was clear of clouds and the heat was causing lines at the ice cream and lemonade stands. He stumbled across a few friends along the way, enjoying catching up with each one.

He found Alex and they walked over to the food court area and grabbed a couple plates of fried chicken, mashed potatoes, and potato salad, and two sodas. They made their way down a grassy hill towards a small pond full of ducks and geese and ate under the large oak tree that hung over the cool waters. When they'd eaten everything on their plates, he pulled Alex into his lap and they watched the ducks swimming and listened to the children rolling down the hill.

Alex looked sexier than ever in her dress outfit, ready for her barrel racing competition. Her hat hung around her neck, and she wore a white shirt, a belt, and boots that were all lined with turquoise beads.

When it was time, they walked up to the main arena, and Grant found Haley in the stands as the first round of competition started. Everyone laughed as they watched the small kids mutton busting. When the barrel racing started, Grant was on the edge of his seat as Alex bolted from barrel to barrel. He'd always been amazed at how fast she rode and how well she and the horse moved as a unit.

At the end of the first competition, Alex was safely in the lead. Grant made his way down to the gate and talked to her as she brushed her horse, Sophie.

They talked until Alex had to ride again. Before leaving, she leaned across the gate and planted a kiss on Grant's lips. He pulled her closer and deepened it, taking his time to explore her mouth and enjoy the taste and feel of her.

She pulled away and walked back over to her horse, smiling and waving at him. He turned around and almost walked into Travis and his folks. Roy and Patty Nolan were some of the highest-class people in town. At least that's what they wanted everyone to think. But the people of Fairplay knew better.

Roy had been the mayor for several terms now, and there was no end in sight. But at home, things weren't as in control. Travis was reckless and had a skill for ending up on the wrong side of the bars at the local jailhouse, and Roy was a pushover. Patty was the one that ruled the house. Maybe that's how Travis had ended up the way he was.

The trio frowned in his direction, and then Roy stepped forward and stretched out his hand for Grant to shake.

"Grant, good to see you. Still sticking around these parts, I see." He laughed.

"Yes, sir. I'm back home to stay." He saw something flash in the man's eyes, but tried to avoid feeling bitter. This was the man who was trying to get his law license revoked, or at least that's what he and his father thought. The complaint had come from the mayor's desk, after all.

"Good, good. You staying with your folks?" Grant could feel Travis' eyes pierce into him, but avoided looking directly at him.

"No, sir. I purchased the old Wilkinson's place late last year."

"Wilkinson's? Out by Saddleback, huh?" There was a spark in the older man's eyes. Then he cleared his throat. "I was just talking to my old buddy down at the state board about that new business you and your daddy are starting up," Roy said with a smile, as his wife coughed. When Grant looked towards her, he could see that her face and neck had turned a deep shade of red.

"Yes, sir. We're real excited about it. My father's been looking forward to getting it up and running. Well..." Grant tipped his hat and tried to excuse himself from the odd situation. When he finally did break free, he walked around the oval arena and sat down next to Chase just as Alex and Sophie came rushing out of the gate.

She shaved four seconds off her last run. The final rounds were set for tomorrow evening, just before the broncos came out.

Alex changed into a jean skirt and blouse, then came out and sat with Grant. They watched the rodeo for another half an hour before heading back to check on his goats. Alex sat with all the girls, brushing them and cuddling with each one. Their ribbon ceremony wasn't until the next day, but Grant and Alex spent some time walking around, looking at all the other animals.

Then they walked hand in hand around the fairgrounds, taking everything in, including the food tent where several of Grant's mother's pies and canned goods had big blue ribbons attached to the nameplates.

After a couple plates each of several different pies and goodies, they made their way across the field towards all the rides just as the hot sun was dipping lower, causing the fall sky to turn a pretty shade of fuchsia. The noise level here easily tripled. It seemed that most of the crowd had followed them here. Little kids ran around with brightly colored balloons tied to their wrists and cotton candy stuck to their faces.

They rode almost every ride. When they rode the Ferris wheel, he pulled her close as it stopped with them at the top. He wrapped his arms around her and dipped his head for a taste. She was sweeter then he'd remembered. He felt her shiver as he pulled her closer and looked down into her deep eyes. He took the kiss deeper and couldn't stop himself from enjoying everything she had to offer.

They didn't notice when the wheel started again, and by the time the attendant was pulling up the gate, they were both breathless and trying to figure out the quickest way back to his truck.

"Hurry," she said as they finally approached his truck in the back parking lot. She pushed his shoulders up against the side of his truck, melting herself against the front of him, using her mouth to heat him even further.

"Alex, my god, you have to slow—" He whispered and then groaned when she slowly undid several of the buttons on his shirt and raked her nails across his stomach muscles. He quickly reversed their positions, pulling her up as he dipped his head and took her lips faster, harder. Their breathing hitched out loudly in the quiet parking lot. The dim lights here gave them plenty of privacy. His boots scraped across the soft grass under their feet as he pushed her legs farther apart so he could stand between them. His hands ran over her hips, pulling her shirt up until he could finally touch her heated skin. Her fingers dug into him, holding, pulling.

When they heard voices, they pulled apart and looked at each other. Alex laughed nervously as she tucked her shirt in. He quickly opened the door for her and helped her into the truck.

When he got behind the wheel, he noticed that his hands were shaking. Instead of starting the truck, he sat there while his knuckles turned white on the steering wheel as he tried to level his breathing.

"Grant?" He could hear the desire in her voice. "I didn't mean...I can't think..." When he looked over at her, he could tell she was as affected as he was. Then she was in his lap as her mouth took his again. His hands raked over her, grabbing at her clothing. He heard something tear and felt satisfaction when finally her skin was exposed for his exploration. She arched as he scooted further into the middle of the large front seat so she could wrap her hips around his. Her tight skirt hiked up her hips. He yanked her panties aside, sinking his fingers into her heat as she moaned.

She fused her mouth to his as her fingers fumbled to release him from his jeans, then she was straddling him again, her soft skin up against his as his hands ran over her silky softness. The windows fogged up as they feasted, moving faster than even he'd ever imagined. Before he could get himself under any kind of control, she was sliding down on his length and swaying those luscious hips to her own internal rhythm. He leaned his head back against the headrest and held on as she drove him a little closer to losing his sanity.

Alex came back to her senses when she heard a couple of car doors slam. When the lights of someone's car flashed for a second into the cab of Grant's truck, she closed her eyes to the brightness and cringed, hoping that some young family hadn't gotten a view of what had happened a few moments before.

He'd destroyed her. All day long, he'd been the perfect gentlemen, opening doors for her, buying her little trinkets at the fair, kissing her softly at the top of the Ferris wheel. She'd never experienced anything like it before. Travis had always been too busy with himself to show her a good time.

In all the years she'd attended the rodeo, she'd never had more fun than she'd had with Grant today.

Cracking her eyes open a little, she looked down at him and smiled. His hair was a mess from her fingers. He was resting his head back and his eyes were closed as he tried to steady his breathing. She could feel his heart beating frantically against her own and smiled a little more. They'd destroyed each other. Satisfaction. Complete and utter satisfaction.

"I've never done that before," he said, without opening his eyes.

She chuckled. "Really?"

"Well, I've done *that*." His eyes opened and she could almost see him blushing in the darkness. "Just not…"

She laughed and leaned down and placed a kiss on his lips. "Me, either."

"Come on," he said when they heard more car doors shutting. "Sounds like the gates are closing. I'd better get you home so you can rest for tomorrow's big event."

When they drove up to the house, Lauren and Chase's truck was already parked under the light.

Grant's eyes stayed focused straight ahead. "Listen, I didn't mean…" He trailed off as he turned towards her. "I mean…We went so fast we forgot…"

She looked at him, her head tilted a little. Then she began to laugh when his meaning finally hit her. He frowned even more until she leaned over and placed a kiss on his lips.

"Don't worry about it. I've been on the pill since I was seventeen and haven't missed a day since." She giggled.

"Oh," he said, frowning a little more. She

thought she'd see relief in his face, but there was none.

"What?" she asked, her smile slowly dipping.

"What?" He looked up at her, "Oh, no, it's nothing." He smiled slowly at her, running his hands over her arms.

"Grant? How long have we known each other?"

His smile was faster this time. "Not long enough, darlin'." He pulled her closer and when he finally let her go, she'd forgotten what she'd been trying to get out of him.

When she walked in the front door, she was surprised to see Haley sitting in the living room with a boy. Alex almost tripped over her feet and had to grab the door frame to keep from falling over.

"Hey," Haley said, looking over the back of the couch. An old movie was playing on the set and the boy's arm was around her sister's shoulders.

"Hey," she replied back, and when the boy turned around, she noticed it was Tom Blake, one of the boys from Haley's class at school. Tom was a good enough guy, but not the kind of guy she'd imagined her sister going for. After all, Haley had been hopelessly devoted to Wes Tanner since grade school. When Wes had left Haley high and dry by joining the Army, she had waited. She hadn't gone out once in all the time he'd been gone, and Lauren and Alex thought their sister would have rather joined a nunnery than try and date anyone else.

So it came as a shock to see Haley and Tom snuggled together on the couch, watching old movies.

"Well, I'm heading up. Night." She rushed up the stairs and stopped at the top, listening for a short while. When she couldn't make out anything, she quietly made her way down the hall and knocked on Lauren and Chase's door.

Chase answered in his boxers, and Alex rushed in the room. Lauren had the sheet tucked around her shoulders. Alex knew she'd interrupted something, but didn't care.

"Did you know that our sister is downstairs with a boy?"

Lauren blinked a few times, shock registering on her face.

"A boy!" Alex repeated and sat next to her sister, hearing Chase sigh as he shut the door.

"Who?" Lauren sat up a little more, adjusting the sheet.

"Tom Blake."

"Tommy Blake? What's she…? I thought…"

"Yeah, me too."

"I didn't know," Lauren said, shaking her head.

"I know, me either. I thought…," Alex started.

"So did I," Lauren said.

They stopped the word game when Chase cleared his throat. "Would someone please tell me what the big deal is? Why does it matter if Haley has a boy downstairs? I happen to know Tom and he's a good guy."

"Oh," Lauren said, waving her hand at her husband. "It's not about who she's with; it's just that she's with someone other than Wes."

"What?" Chase walked over and grabbed his pants and pulled them on quickly.

"Wes Tanner," Lauren said. "Haley's one and only Prince Charming."

"Wes is in Iraq or Afghanistan somewhere, I can't remember where just now. But I've heard that he hasn't been back in town for almost three years now."

"We know," Alex said, then turned back to her sister. "Do you think this means...?"

"I don't know, we'll just have to wait and see," Lauren broke in and answered her unasked question.

"Ugh, I give up. I'm going to go get a drink of water." Chase started heading towards the door, but both women yelled at him.

"No!"

"Honey, grab a drink from the bathroom. Let's give Haley some privacy," Lauren said, smiling.

Chase shrugged his shoulders and walked into

the adjoining bathroom.

That night Alex lay in bed thinking of Grant. Her mind flashed to what he'd been hinting at. She'd seen it in his eyes. She'd known him forever and thought she knew what he was thinking. He'd been sad about the possibility of not having kids with her.

No, she told herself. There was no way he was thinking that far ahead. She was only twenty-four, and he was just a month older. They weren't even really an official item. More like just distractions. Friends helping each other out, right? Maybe she'd forgotten to tell him that's how she saw their relationship. Maybe she should have set some boundaries before they'd gotten started. After all, she'd just gotten out of a long-term relationship and was not looking for anything permanent.

Besides, Grant wasn't her type. Well, not for the long run. He was way too nice; she'd just end up hurting him. Right? He was such an honest guy. She couldn't think of anything wrong with that other than the fact that it used to annoy her in school.

She wasn't good enough for him. She knew it and probably the whole town knew it, too. She was a waitress at a run-down diner. She had no real prospects of a future. She hadn't even changed that much over the years. She was the same old Alex.

Grant wasn't the same kid he'd been in school. He wasn't the same kid outside either. She remembered running her hands over his tight body earlier that night in his truck. How his muscles had jumped and flexed under her fingers. His skin was toned and tan thanks to the hard work he did outside in the sun. It had even lightened his hair, giving him a beach-bum-meets-rough-cowboy look.

He was smart, responsible, kind, sexy, and damn good in bed. Adding it all up, Alex started wondering why she still felt she had to talk herself out of thinking about Grant in a long-term sort of way. She still felt like there was something holding her back, she just couldn't put her finger on what it was.

Jill Sanders

Chapter Fourteen

Grant had missed her last night and knew that his bed would be lonely again tonight, since she had plans to celebrate with her family after the big fireworks show. He also had plans to spend time with his family. He had cousins coming into town later today and knew that his parents' house would be full by nightfall.

So when he spotted Alex across the parking lot at the fairgrounds, he rushed over to talk to her.

"Alex," he called and smiled when she stopped and turned to him. But when a slight frown appeared on her lips, he almost stopped. He jogged up next to her and looked down at her. "What's wrong?" He pulled her close, looking into her dark eyes. He could see shadows under them and wondered if something had happened.

"It's nothing." She shook her head and tried to

smile at him, but her eyes showed that she was still thinking of something else.

He pulled her aside, just outside the entry gate, and walked her into the shade where they could talk alone.

"Something's wrong," he said, running his hands up and down her arms.

She sighed and looked at him. "I think I need a break," she said, not looking into his eyes, focusing on a button on his chest.

"A break?" he asked, feeling his heart skip a beat.

She nodded. "Yeah, I need some time to think about things. I'm thinking of going to my cousins' for a while. I think I just need to get away for a while." She gently pulled her hands out of his, removing all doubt in his mind of what she meant.

"Time?" he said, feeling his heart skip again. Hell, he was sure it had just broken in two. He didn't know what to say. Had he not taken the time and told her how he felt? Maybe she didn't know? And after last night! Maybe he'd done something wrong? "Listen Alex, if I've done something…"

He broke off when she started to shake her head. "No, of course not. You've been…" She sighed. "Wonderful." Her eyes darted over his shoulder. He turned in time to see her sister walking towards them, hand in hand with Tom Blake. Alex frowned even more. "Listen, I have to go get ready." She turned and started walking away, and he felt like his whole world was crashing down on him.

He walked to the goat section, not really seeing anything or hearing anyone. When he got there, he leaned against the gate and would have continued staring off into space if Mojo hadn't been adamant about getting in his face.

"What?" he finally asked her after she'd head-butted him for the tenth time. "I'll get you your damn breakfast." He turned to go get some grain, when he noticed there were only two kids in the corral with her.

"Where's Buttercup?" he asked Mojo, half expecting the goat to answer him. He went down the first row, looking in every pen, searching for the lost goat. After he'd searched the whole barn, every corral, he started enlisting help. An hour later, everyone was on the lookout for Buttercup. After two hours, he'd worked himself into a frantic state; his baby was gone.

The plans were ruined. It was all over the fair grounds that she'd broken up with Grant. Panic settled in. Then a peace fell as a new scene unfolded. Grant was walking towards the large barn where Alex was. Maybe this could be a little fun after all.

213

Alex found it very hard to concentrate. She was up next and her eyes still burned. She'd spent most of last night going over how much better off Grant would be without her. She'd just hold him back. She was trouble. She'd known it her whole life. It was her fault that their mother had gone back inside after Haley. She'd distracted Lauren long enough that Haley had slipped away. She would be a distraction to Grant, she just knew it. His internet business and farm needed his full attention. He had a future. Plans.

She shook her head clear and prepared herself for the run. Sophie nervously jolted under her when the buzzer sounded, and she tucked her knees and held on as the horse ran its programed pattern. When they flew across the gate, she knew that she'd gained time instead of shaving it off. Closing her eyes as Sophie came to a halt, she looked over at the scoreboard and sighed. Five seconds gained.

Waiting for the other ladies to take their turns, she took her time brushing down Sophie and preparing the horse for the ride home later that night. Chase, Lauren, and Haley would all help load up Sophie and Haley's blue-ribbon steer after everyone left for the night.

As she was cooling the horse down, Travis walked up to her and leaned on the post. "Heard you broke up with Holton. Decided he wasn't man enough for you?" Travis leaned over and flipped a piece of her hair out of her eyes.

"Something like that." She jolted away, not wanting to give him any time. He moved closer and pinned her in the stall.

"Well, if you decide you'd like me back..." He leaned down as she pushed him away, the horse brush still gripped firmly in her hands.

"Back off," she said under her breath.

He pulled her hips towards him and she could feel he was hard, causing a shiver to race up her spine. He smelled of booze and cigarettes, a scent that caused her stomach to turn. She pushed him even harder, wedging the sharp brush between them.

"Come on, Alex. We both know you were just toying with Mr. Goody Two-shoes."

Before she could say anything, she looked over and saw Grant standing at the end of the stall. He'd clearly heard what Travis had just said. Grant's blue eyes looked hollow and the look on his face told her he believed it all.

Before she could yell for him, he took off, walking quickly down the lane. Travis laughed when he saw Grant walk away.

"Serves him right. Now he knows what it's like

to have your woman taken away from you." He tried to pull her closer.

"You idiot," she screamed. "I am not your woman. You're the one that cheated on me, you son of a bitch!" She kicked out and caught him in the chin, hurting him enough that he loosened his vice-like hold on her. Shoving the wire brush between them, she kicked out again.

By the time she finally freed herself from Travis' hold, Grant was nowhere to be found. She ran out of the barn and started searching for him.

It was midday and everyone was outside trying to find someplace to eat. The booths and tents that lined the food court were packed. She could hardly wade through the growing crowd of hungry people. She searched everywhere for Grant. She swung by the goat barn. He wasn't there, but she saw a sign posted to the gate about Buttercup. Her heart skipped. Buttercup was missing. He'd probably come to ask her for help looking for the lost goat.

Finally, she headed towards his truck to leave him a note. She was walking through the parking lot packed with trucks and trailers when she heard bleating. She approached the trailer and looked in the dark windows, but couldn't see anything. Getting up on the wheel well, she looked inside the bigger window and saw Buttercup butting the door.

Jumping down, she rushed over to the door and

yanked it opened. The young goat looked at her like she was thinking it was about time she got there. A shadow fell over them, and when Alex turned to see what it was, a light exploded on the left side of her head followed quickly by darkness.

Jill Sanders

Chapter Fifteen

Grant rushed out of the building, not really seeing where he was going. When he ran into someone, he apologized quickly and continued walking until he ended up at the lake under the tall oak tree where he and Alex had picnicked the day before. He sat down in the shade and thought about the turn of events.

Where had he gone wrong? He folded his knees up and placed his elbows on them, watching two young boys throw rocks into the water.

"Hey." He jumped at the voice behind him. When he looked, Haley stood looking down at him. "Can I sit with you?"

He nodded, and she sat next to him, crossing her legs and watching the kids.

"I heard about what happened between you and

Alex," she said, not looking in his direction.

He turned to her, and the scene that he'd just witnessed of Alex in Travis' arms as they'd laughed at him played over in his head.

"That she'd broken it off with you this morning," she said, letting him know what she'd been talking about.

He nodded and looked down at his hands.

"My sister can be stupid." She smiled at him and placed a gentle hand on his arm. "Listen, I know her and can tell you without question that you're the best thing that has ever happened to her."

He laughed, harshly. "I doubt that." He shook his head, looking back at the water. To think he'd been thinking about settling down with her. Raising a family.

"I know it can be hard to understand"—she pulled his arm until he looked at her again—"but she needs you. Travis broke her. Not physically, but emotionally. She was so rundown, she didn't think she knew what she wanted. In the last few months since she's been seeing you, for the first time in a long time she has a purpose. She's been focused. She was hurt when Travis cheated on her, but because of you, she forgot about him. Forgot about any other man that had come before."

"Apparently not enough. I just caught them together."

220

"What?" Haley's hand jerked on his arm. "Alex and Travis?"

He nodded.

"You idiot!" Haley stood up and looked towards the barn. She looked down at him with a scowl. "I suppose you just left her there to defend herself."

He stood and thought about it. Closing his eyes, he remembered how they'd been standing in the stall and the truth hit him full force. Travis had had Alex cornered. Her arms had been up against his chest in defense, trying to push him away. Anger and fear had been written on her face.

Haley was right; he'd been such an idiot.

Opening his eyes, he looked down at Haley. "You know, you're pretty smart." He pulled her braid and rushed off towards the barn, hoping he wasn't too late for an apology.

When he didn't find Alex in Sophie's stall, he rushed to the goat corral and asked around. She'd been there five minutes before he had. Following directions from a few people, he rushed out to the parking lot to look for her.

He was just about to give up when he spotted the wire horse brush. It had been crunched under a tire, but he knew it was hers. It was the same bright pink one she'd been holding against Travis' chest.

He started yelling for her. He couldn't explain the urgency he felt to find her, other than the fact that he wanted to apologize for being a fool and to see if she was okay after being left alone to deal with Travis. He'd called her a few more times when Haley, Lauren, and Chase all rushed out to the parking lot.

"Did you find her yet?" Lauren asked, looking around.

"No. Someone said she came out here about ten minutes ago. I found this." He held it out.

"That's Alex's," Haley said, then called out to her sister. They spread out, calling her name until Chase finally yelled, "Over here. She's over here."

Everyone rushed over. Grant was breathless when he arrived at the trailer. His trailer. He saw her in an unconscious ball with Buttercup snuggled next to her. He would have thought the scene was endearing if it hadn't been for the large bump growing on her forehead. A bruise was forming there and there was a trickle of blood dripping slowly down her forehead.

He rushed to her side. Chase was there checking her vitals. He swatted him aside and pulled her into his lap, calling her name over and over again. Her eyelids slowly opened as he watched her. He saw her try to focus on his fingers as he pushed a strand of her hair aside.

Looking up he realized they had an audience, now. The sheriff, the mayor, and the mayor's family stood just outside his trailer, looking in on the scene.

"What's going on here?" The sheriff jumped up in the back of the trailer and looked down at Alex.

"It looks like someone knocked her over the head," Grant said, then noticed the tire iron lying next to him. "Probably with that." He nodded.

"Has someone called an ambulance?" the sheriff asked.

"I did," Lauren said with a shaky voice. Haley and Lauren were sitting on the other side of their sister, as Alex focused on them.

"What?" she asked, trying to sit up.

"Don't," Chase said, holding her still. "Hold still, sweetie. Where does it hurt?"

"I feel like I've been bucked off a bronco and landed on my head. What happened?" She grabbed her head with her hands and moaned.

"We were hoping you could tell us." Lauren leaned over her sister.

"I don't really remember. I came out here to find Grant and heard Buttercup crying." She pulled the goat into her lap again where it snuggled up to her. "Then I don't remember."

"Well, isn't it obvious?" It was Travis that spoke. Everyone turned to look at him. Grant hadn't even noticed that he'd been standing right there with his family. He looked around and shrugged his shoulders and nodded towards them. "Everyone knows they had a fight earlier today and broke up. Plus, he caught us in the barn just a while ago. It's obvious Grant couldn't take it and he followed her out here, hitting her over the head. She is in his trailer. It is his tire iron."

"You've got to be kidding me!" It was Haley who spoke this time. She slowly stood up. "First of all, we all know you've been stalking Alex since your break up four months ago. Not to mention all the terrible things you've done to Grant here. Second of all, Grant was with me fifteen minutes ago, across the fairgrounds by the lake. He was a minute ahead of us walking into the parking lot." She looked to Lauren and Chase for confirmation, and they both nodded in agreement.

"Well, I'm not taking the blame for this one. Not this time. I was in line to get some barbeque just a few minutes ago. My dad and the sheriff here pulled me out, saying we were heading to Mama's with the sheriff instead."

"He's right," the sheriff piped in. "We all saw him standing in line. He was second in line to be served out of around ten. He'd been there a while." The sheriff looked down at Grant. "Well, for now, let's get Alex checked out and we can debate who took part in what later." They all looked up as the ambulance drove up.

Grant rode with Lauren and Chase in their truck, while Haley road with Alex in the ambulance. The entire drive to the clinic, everyone sat in silence, the same question running through everyone's mind. Who had done this?

It took almost an hour for Alex to come back out front after seeing the doctor. Grant had sat in the small waiting room with Chase since the doctor's room was too small and only family members were allowed back with the patients.

When they wheeled her out, she had small white bandages over her forehead. Her eyes were closed, but when Grant said her name, she opened them and frowned a little.

"I can't..." She shook her head and moaned. "Please." She looked up at Haley, who nodded to her sister, then walked towards him. Taking his arm, she steered him out the door and told him.

"Grant, I tried to talk to her, but she won't listen." She looked back inside and shook her head. "Stubborn." Then she sighed. "Listen, I'll try again later. It's best if you give her some time. Just give her a day, let her head get clear of all this."

He nodded, not really taking it all in. "Is she going to be okay?"

"Yeah." She sighed again. "No stitches, just a slight concussion. We're supposed to watch her for a while."

"Can I do...?" he started, but stopped when she shook her head no.

"No, she doesn't want anything right now."

They both looked up when Grant's parents walked up. "We just heard." His mother rushed to his side. "Is Alex okay?" she asked Haley.

"Yes." Haley took his mother's hand and walked her inside to see Alex, who was still sitting in the wheelchair, waiting to be released.

"What a shame. Sounds like someone's gone too far this time."

"Hmmm." He was only half-listening to his father.

"I heard they stole your goat, the one that won the blue ribbon."

"What?" He looked over and watched as her family wheeled her out to Chase's truck.

"Your goat. I know it's not the time, but do you think someone attacked her to steal your blue ribbon goat?"

"My goat didn't win," he said, absently.

"Sure it did. That little one they found in the trailer with Alex. Everyone's saying it won the highest award, best in show."

He turned and looked at his dad. "Buttercup won?"

His dad nodded and smiled, then when he looked over at Alex, his smile fell away. "I sure hope that had nothing to do with your goat."

By the time Grant got all four goats home, including his award-winning Buttercup, trophy and all, he was so tired he couldn't see straight.

He'd messaged Alex several times, but hadn't heard anything back. He'd been such a fool and he knew that he had to make it up to her. By the time the sun finally rose, he thought he had a plan firmly in hand. There was no way she could say no, not after what he had planned. Now he just needed to convince her to talk to him.

Alex lay in bed and watched TV with the sound off. She looked down at her phone when it beeped for the hundredth time since last night. She hadn't even read Grant's first messages, and quickly avoided looking at this one as well.

She thought about turning it off, but she wanted to know that he was suffering like she was. Not just physically, but emotionally.

Oh, she knew she was the one who'd called it all off, or tried to. She'd been a fool trying to think she could have a normal life. She wasn't good enough for someone like Grant. She'd done some real soul searching last night after she'd gotten home and had laid it all out. She was a waitress at a greasy diner. She had no real skills and no idea what she wanted to do in the future. Grant was a Harvard graduate with a law degree and a smart business plan. Not to mention a house of his own and definite plans for his future.

The only thing she had in her future was...

well, nothing she could think of. That's why she'd decided that she was leaving to go see her cousins. She could stay with them for a while and make up her mind as to what her next step was. She had a little money saved up; it might even be enough to take some night classes.

She'd started packing up her things early that morning so she could move back into her old room. They could redecorate the larger room for the baby. She was thinking about just storing all of her things up in the attic. That way she would only have to take a small suitcase with her.

Getting off the bed slowly, she tested the waters to see how she felt. When her vision grayed just a little, she closed her eyes and took several deep breaths. Her head had hurt her most of the day and her sisters had locked her in her room, delivering her food and checking up on her. Haley had been upset when she'd seen her packing boxes. She said that Alex was supposed to be resting, but Alex had ignored her and only stopped when she felt dizzy. Now the sun was setting and she was getting tired of being in her room alone. When she opened her eyes again, she let out a loud scream.

On the other side of her window was a face. She didn't stop screaming until she realized the face belonged to Grant. Then she rushed to her window and opened it quickly.

"What in the hell are you doing? Don't you know it's a fifteen-foot drop?" She held onto his hands and looked out the window. He was standing on a silver ladder. A very tall silver ladder.

Just then Lauren and Chase came rushing in her room. Chase held a baseball bat, ready to bash someone's head in. Lauren had her trusty revolver, cocked and ready to shoot whatever or whoever had caused her sister to scream so loud.

"What is going on?" they both asked at the same time.

"It's okay," Alex said, holding her hands up, laughing. "I'm okay."

When they noticed Grant's head poking in through the window, they both relaxed.

"You have a very scary wife," Grant said, hoisting himself over the windowsill and looking down at the gun in Lauren's hand. Chase turned and noticed the gun just as Lauren released the hammer.

Chase laughed. "You have no idea what that one hides under *her* bed," he said, pointing at Alex. He nodded to Grant, then turned his wife around and marched her out of the room.

Lauren called out over her shoulder, "If you need help, just holler." Chase closed the door behind him.

"Are you going somewhere?" Grant asked, looking around her room.

She turned back to him, her arms crossed over her chest. "Yes." Her head was feeling light from all the excitement, so she walked over and sat down on the edge of her bed. "I'm going to my cousins', remember."

He looked around again. "Forever?"

She shrugged her shoulders.

"Because of me?" He walked over and sat next to her.

She refused to look at him. If she looked into those deep blue eyes, she might lose her nerve. Going away was for the best. For both of them.

"Alex, would you please look at me?" he asked, taking her chin with just a finger and pulling it towards him.

She closed her eyes and sighed. "I can't. I can't do this." She kept her eyes closed tight.

"I'm sorry," he said softly. Then his weight lifted from the mattress. She kept her eyes closed tight and heard him walk back towards the window. She listened carefully but didn't hear him leave, so she peeked out one eye and watched as he leaned out the window.

"What are you doing?" she asked, folding her arms across her chest.

"I have something for you, but the rope is stuck," he said, grunting a little.

"Unless you're going to hang yourself"—she turned away from the window and smiled—"you better just take whatever it is back. I don't want anything from you."

"There," he said, ignoring her. "Got it. Here we go," he said as he pulled on the rope, leaving a heap of it lying on her bedroom floor alongside her boxes.

Her curiosity finally got the better of her and she walked over to the window in time to see him pull a small basket tied securely with the rope through her window.

"What is it?" she asked, leaning against her windowsill.

"You'll have to promise to listen to me. To let me speak and talk to you first."

She shook her head, but couldn't put a lot of feeling behind it.

"Alex?" He looked down at her and held the basket to his side, turning his shoulders so she couldn't see it.

"Fine!" She threw up her hands in frustration. How did he know she had a weakness for surprises? She was sure that was all Haley's doing; her sister couldn't keep her mouth shut. "I'll listen to you, but if I don't like what you have to say, you and whatever is in the basket will go out the window, without the use of the ladder." She crossed her arms over her chest again.

He smiled. "Fair enough." Then he turned and handed her the basket. At first she thought he'd given her a brown towel, but then it moved and she almost dropped the basket in shock. His hands came under hers to steady them, then he gently lifted the puppy from the basket and handed it to her.

"You bought me a puppy?" she asked, looking down at the brown blob.

"I bought *us* a puppy," he said, smiling at her.

She stared at him. "You think that by buying me a puppy, you'll make everything bad, everything wrong between us go away?"

He frowned and looked down at his feet. "No, of course not. I thought of Junior here as a peace offering and a means of getting my foot in the window, I mean door." He looked up and smiled a little, causing her heart to skip.

How had he gotten past her defenses so quickly? She'd prepared herself for this, or so she'd told herself. She tried to hand the small bundle back to him, but he crossed his arms and shook his head.

"I'm not doing this." She walked over and set the happy puppy on her bed where it started sniffing around and chewing on her quilt.

"Alex, I only needed to talk to you. Honest. If after ten minutes you don't like what I've said, you can kick me and Junior out. Deal?"

She tried not to melt when his blue eyes turned sad and begging. She sighed and sat next to the dog who immediately climbed up on her lap. She gathered him up and started to pet his soft baby fur as Grant started pacing in front of her.

"Well, let's start at the beginning." He turned and looked down at her. "Eighteen years ago—" he began but stopped when she sighed and glanced up at him. He nodded then continued. "Eighteen years ago, I walked in and caught you stealing a horse. You know in Texas you can still be hung for that crime." He gave her a weak smile, then continued. "You were wearing a yellow sun dress, your hair was in two braids down your back, and the sun was behind you." He stopped his pacing long enough to look at her again, sadness in his eyes. "I lost my heart in aisle three at the Grocery Stop that day. I would have given you anything at that moment. Then you gave me my very first kiss and I knew what I wanted in life. I wanted to someday become worthy of having Alexis West, the girl of my dreams."

She felt like laughing and crying at the same time. How could she have known? But what was she going to do with this knowledge? Before she could say anything, he continued.

"Then in a flash we were in middle school, then junior high, and I was standing in the corner at the dance watching you dance with every boy but me. In high school you were there to stop the kids from calling me names, and you were kind to me even though I was the class nerd and the chubbiest kid in school. I went away to college, all along thinking that I'd come back into town and show you that I was worthy of being with you. Every time I came home from the gym after Sam had destroyed me during a session, I thought of you.

Of being with you." He squatted down in front of her. "Alex, I've loved you since the first grade. I want to keep on loving you. Yesterday morning, when you broke it off, I kind of went insane." He frowned and shook his head. "Then when I saw you with Travis and heard what he said, I felt, for just a moment, that what he was saying was true. Remember, pleading insanity here." He smiled and took one of her hands. "I was wrong. I should have trusted my gut and not my knee-jerk instinct. Can you ever forgive me?"

Tears were lightly flowing down her cheeks, and he reached up with one gentle finger and brushed it aside. She didn't trust herself to speak, so she just nodded her head.

"Good, now comes the difficult part." He took a deep breath and clasped her other hand. "Alexis West, would you do me the honor of moving in with me?"

Her heart had skipped for a fraction of a moment. No! her mind screamed. Not again. She was not going to get engaged again, and so soon. But then she replayed his words. Move in with me. She didn't know what to say. She'd tried the engagement thing, but this wasn't getting married, and it wasn't Travis. Looking up into Grant's blue eyes, she knew without a doubt that he'd never cheat on her, he'd never raise a voice or hand towards her. Besides, he'd just proclaimed that he'd loved her since she was seven. How could she not say yes? Then it dawned on her. That had been the

234

one thing missing. The knowledge of her feelings for him. The idea of getting used to someone day and night. Did she love him? She knew she hadn't loved Travis. She'd thought she'd loved him, but basically she'd tolerated him to get what she wanted: marriage.

Was she going to use Grant that way as well? No. The answer slammed into her head. Blinking back the tears, she knew her answer. Knew that she'd loved him since the night he'd picked her up on side of the road and been kind to her. Since that first real kiss many months ago, when he'd knocked her socks off. He was the only man that made her stutter and feel shy. He was the only one she could see herself growing old with.

"That's a long break there." He smiled nervously at her.

"That was a pretty heavy question you asked." She smiled and nodded. "But I've thought it through, and I have some things to say first." She handed him the puppy and started pacing, much like he had.

"First I need to know, why me? I'm nothing special. I work in a greasy diner and have no real education like you do. I'm stubborn and will always demand I get my way."

He smiled and nodded. "You're twice as smart as most women I met at Harvard. More beautiful than all of them. And I love that you're stubborn. I look forward to giving you everything you'll ever want."

She smiled. "Smooth talker."

He chuckled at her. "Any more questions?"

She thought about it. "If I agree to move in with you…" She paused and could tell he was holding his breath. "We are not naming him Junior."

He blinked, then laughed and jumped off the bed to hug her, the tiny dog squashed lightly between them.

Chapter Sixteen

When they walked downstairs an hour later and entered the kitchen, everyone was there. They were all sitting around the table drinking coffee and looking very worried.

"We didn't hear anything breaking," Chase said and then smiled. He was rewarded with a light kick under the table from his wife.

"Oh, look." Haley got up and rushed over to take the small puppy from Alex's hands.

"It's okay," Alex said. "We're okay." She took Grant's hand and smiled at him. "I'm moving in with Grant."

Everyone was quiet for a second as it sunk in, then they flooded them with congratulations and hugs. Everyone told them how happy they were for them.

Since Alex had to work the next morning, she packed a few things into a large bag that Grant carried out to his truck. The puppy, whom she was thinking of calling Romeo, was tucked in her lap fast asleep as she followed Grant to his house in her car.

When they arrived, he carried her bags inside, turned to her, and wrapped her in his arms. "Welcome home." He kissed her gently on her lips, melting the last part of her defenses.

The next morning his alarm went off early and she flipped the pillow over her head. She could have ignored the alarm and the sound of Grant whistling in the shower, but when the puppy started whining, she wrapped the robe around her and slipped on some shoes to let the little guy go out.

When she opened the back sliding door, she noticed the sun was just coming up. Her eyes weren't all the way open yet as she watched the beautiful colors flood the sky over the fall leaves. Romeo did his business, then shook off the morning dew that he'd rolled in and came in the door. He sat on his bottom and looked up at her.

"I suppose you'll want some breakfast now." She walked into the kitchen and scooped out a cup of food and dumped it into the new dog bowl Grant had purchased for him. The name Junior was scribbled in elegant letters, but Alex knew she would get the final word on his name.

She flipped the coffee maker on just as Grant walked into the kitchen. He walked over to her and wrapped her in his arms, giving her a kiss that told her she was right where she belonged.

Just before noon, she was wondering why she hadn't called in sick at the diner. Her head was throbbing and on several occasions, she'd had to sit down while taking someone's order. Jamella kept trying to convince her to go home, but she had wanted to stick it out until Grant and his parents came by for lunch around twelve thirty. They were going to tell his parents together that she'd moved in with him. When Travis' parents came in a few minutes later, she wished she'd taken Jamella's advice.

"Good morning. Do you know what you want to order?" She tried to give them a big smile. She knew what everyone was seeing when they looked at her. The left side of her forehead was still swollen and there was a butterfly bandage covering a small cut. The bruise that ran from her hairline to just below her left eye looked nasty this morning, so she could only imagine what it looked like now. Even though she'd expertly covered it with makeup, she could tell by the way people were looking at her that they could still see most of it.

"Should you be working in your condition?" Patty Nolan looked down her nose at Alex. Patty had always looked prim and proper. Even when she was working in the yard, the woman never had a hair out of place. Her perfectly manicured nails, her pristine clothing, even her hair was never out of place. Alex cringed when she thought of what she might look like now.

"I'm fine." She smiled and asked if she could take their order again.

"I don't know," Patty said, setting down her menu. "From what I've heard, you've had a lot going on. Is it true that you're going to be moving? Something about going to your cousins'?" She looked at her through squinted eyes. There was a twisted smile on her face, and Alex felt a shiver run down her spine.

"Oh," Roy piped in, "is it true? Are you leaving Fairplay?" There was a sparkle in his eye as well, and Alex felt all the air being sucked out of the room.

"No." She'd known it would travel all over town, since she'd pretty much screamed it at Grant the other day at the fairgrounds. But she hadn't thought about having to explain that she was now living with him. "No, I'm staying in Fairplay."

She watched as both of their faces sank and felt steam coming off her skin. How dare these two make her feel inferior. It was almost as if they'd been happy to hear that she'd be leaving. Well, let them choke on this bit of news.

"Actually, I've moved in with Grant." She smiled big when she saw both of their chins drop.

"Grant? But we heard…," Patty started, only to

be hushed by her husband.

"I suppose it's not true either that you're pregnant?" Roy asked.

Alex looked between the pair. The night Savannah had approached her at the Rusty Rail popped into her head. She couldn't help it, she laughed so hard several people turned their heads.

"No wonder everyone's been looking at me funny all week." She laughed harder, holding her sides. "No," she said loudly, "I'm not expecting. But I'm happy to say that Lauren and Chase will be welcoming their first child early next summer." There, let the town choke on that.

"Now, would you like to order something or did you just come in here to hear the latest gossip about my life?" She smiled even more when she saw Patty's face start to turn purple. "I'll give you two a few more minutes to look over the menu, shall I?" She turned on her heel and walked away without another word.

Walking into the back, she waited until the door swung shut, then collapsed into Jamella's relaxin' chair just inside her office.

"What da say to you dat has you upset?" Jamella walked in and took the seat across from her.

"Nothing." She closed her eyes for a moment, wishing the throbbing would subside just a little. "Jamella? Am I smart?"

"What kind o' question is dat? Of course you're

241

smart. You da smartest girl I knowed. Why do you tink I kept you on so long?"

She shrugged her shoulders.

"Did da tell you dat you weren't smart?" She watched her boss rise no doubt to go and tell the mayor and his wife off.

"Hang on." She took her arm and held her still. "No, they didn't. It's just that I've always thought of myself as just ordinary. I mean…" She dropped her hand and looked down at her fingers. "I did okay in school. Made good grades and all, but I never went to college. I've only been to two major cities my whole life. I've actually never even been outside of Texas. I'm just afraid that Grant deserves someone better. Someone smarter." She sighed.

"Girl, none of dat stuff matters. You have what matters, in here." She tapped her chest and lightly put her fingers against her forehead. "And in here. Girl, you are like my own, you and your sisters. My kids…" She grunted and shook her head. "Mmm, dey took off and left me alone to all dis. But, you…" She looked down at her. "You walked in dat day and filled a spot in my heart." She patted her chest. "Girl, you are worth eighty times any girl dat went to a fancy school." She pulled her up and gave her a big hug. "Now, stick dat chin in da air." She smiled when Alex did. "Good, girl."

"Thanks, Jamella. Your kids don't know what they are missing." She placed a kiss on the woman's wet cheek and walked out front feeling better.

By the time Grant and his family walked in, Travis' parents had left. She was thankful for that and sat down next to Grant.

"You look tired," he said, frowning. "How's the head?" He brushed a strand of her hair away from her eyes.

"I'm okay, now that you're here." She leaned over and kissed him right there.

"You two look good together," his mother said, leaning against his father's shoulder. "Don't they dear?"

"Yes, I always knew you would get together." He smiled then laughed when his wife gently hit him in the arm.

"Alex is moving in with me," Grant said, smiling at Alex. "Oh, and you have a grandson." Grant laughed when his mother's face turned a little pale.

"A puppy grandson," Alex corrected and slapped Grant's shoulder. "Don't scare your folks like that.

"Scare? My dear, I was excited. But a puppy will do for now." She smiled.

She had laughed at them. Actually laughed at them in front of everyone at Mama's. How dare she do that. How dare she ruin everything. Well, there was only one way to handle this now. Looking down at what lay in the seat, a smile crept across lips slowly.

Taking everything she loved away from her would prove to her that she wasn't worthy. Maybe then she would leave and never return. Maybe then she would understand that you don't screw around with the Nolans.

Grant convinced Alex to head home with him after lunch. She'd really looked too tired to continue her shift, and he could tell that she had a headache. After his parents left, he stuck around until she closed out then drove her home in his truck since she looked too tired to drive herself. He told her they'd get her car first thing in the morning. She closed her eyes and rested her head all the way home. Their home. He still couldn't get used to it. He knew this was just step one in his master plan to convince her to marry him by Christmas.

Alex was down the hall, taking a nap, and Grant worked on the website, answering emails from clients, since his license had been fully approved. He'd fallen into a pattern of spending a few hours a day answering questions. He actually found it very enjoyable and looked forward to getting more clients. His father helped out and took his share of questions every day as well.

The doorbell rang, and Junior started yapping. Grant quickly scooped the little guy up before he could wake Alex. "Shhh," he told him as he walked to the door. "Hush now or you'll wake your mother. Shall we see who's come to visit us?" He held the small dog to his chest.

When he opened the door, he was smiling and had no time to react. He saw the smoke at the bottom of the stairs first. It billowed out in a white puff, fogging his view. Then he heard the loud crack as the air was ripped apart. He hit the ground before he felt any pain. All he could feel was sorrow for what he knew was coming next for Alex.

Alex jumped when she heard the loud crack.

245

Her eyes darted open as she sat up in bed. Her foggy mind wondered if she'd just dreamed it, then she heard frantic yapping and rushed down the hall. She stood at the end of the hallway, frozen as she looked at the horror that lay before her.

Grant was flat on his back, his feet at the edge of the doorway. There was a fist-sized hole in his shirt and blood slowly oozed out of the hole. Rushing to the front door, she clasped a hand over Grant's chest, trying to stop the bleeding, which by now covered the whole front of his shirt.

When she heard gravel being thrown by tires, she looked out the door in time to see a blue truck speed out their driveway.

"Grant!" she screamed over and over, not knowing what to do. She kept her hands over his chest as his face and arms drained of color. With shaky hands, she reached for his cell phone on the table by the front door. It was charging and she fought with the cable as she tried to pull it closer so she could keep pressure on his chest.

When she dialed, blood splattered the screen from her fingers, causing her to dial slowly. She felt his chest rise and fall sporadically and closed her eyes for a moment, shooting up the mother of all prayers.

When she set the phone down, still on speakerphone with 911, she noticed Romeo was lying by Grant's side. The little dog was breathing hard as blood oozed slowly out of his hip. Keeping pressure on Grant's chest, she reached over and started putting pressure on his wound as well.

Hours later, she rushed into the waiting room at Mother Frances Hospital in Tyler. They had Life-Flighted Grant to the hospital from their front yard.

It had taken Alex, Lauren, and Haley almost an hour to get there by car. Chase had stayed behind to see to the dog with a promise that he'd be there as soon as he could. She couldn't stop shaking. She was still covered in blood, some of it Romeo's.

Concern for the dog hadn't even registered yet, since her mind was completely focused on Grant. He'd lost so much blood. Had the bullet hit his heart? So many questions ran through her mind. Haley had tried to keep her from shaking by holding her hand, but Alex just rocked back and forth instead.

When they arrived, Grant's parents were already there. Worry flashed in their faces when they saw how much blood was still on her hands and arms. She'd changed her clothes in the car, thanks to Haley having a spare pair of jeans and a sweatshirt in the back of the truck. But her hands and arms were still covered with the blood she'd tried to keep from leaving his body.

"Where is he?" She rushed into the emergency room.

"They have him in surgery," they said together. Tears streamed down their faces. "What happened?" Carolyn asked.

She had quickly told the sheriff what she'd seen while the ambulance crew worked on Grant as they waited for the helicopter to pick him up. She'd told him who she'd seen leaving their house, but it still hadn't fully sunk in.

"It was Travis' mother. Patty Nolan did this," she whispered, shaking her head. "I saw her driving away in Travis' truck." She shook her head again as tears rolled down her cheeks.

"Patty?" Carolyn said, "No." She shook her head. "It couldn't have been Patty." She grabbed her husband's arm.

"Why?" Glenn asked, walking his wife over and helping her sit down. "Why?" he asked again.

"I think it was to get back at me," she said softly as her sisters took her arms and forced her to sit. "It's all my fault."

"No," Haley and Lauren said at the same moment. They looked at each other.

"No," Lauren said again. "You didn't do anything wrong. I don't know why Patty Nolan did this, but I'm sure it is not your fault."

"She's right," Glenn said as he rubbed his wife's shoulders. "If he hadn't talked you into leaving work early, he'd be gone." His voice hitched. "You were there. Your quick response saved our son. The paramedics told us so." He smiled a little.

"How do you know?" She stood up and threw up her arms. "If he wasn't seeing me, none of this would have happened." She stormed out of the waiting room, blindly heading down hall after hall of the unfamiliar hospital. She could hear her sisters calling after her so she ducked into a dark room. She held her breath when they passed her hiding spot, calling out to her.

Closing her eyes, she rested her head back against the door and tried to level her breathing. But when her breath hitched, she collapsed against the door and cried.

"Oh, what's the matter dear?" came a sweet voice.

Looking up through watery eyes, she noticed she was in someone's private hospital room.

"Oh!" She blinked and wiped her eyes. "I'm sorry. I didn't know..." She looked around.

"It's okay, dear. Come over here." The frail gray-haired woman patted her bed. "Don't be shy. I stopped biting after they took my teeth away." She smiled and Alex saw that the woman was completely toothless. She couldn't even smile at the joke.

"What's the matter? What has such a pretty young thing like you crying like the world has just ended?"

"It has," she said, her voice hitching as she walked closer to the woman's bed. Then everything came out. The whole story from how she'd been the cause of her mother's death to how she was to blame for Grant. Everything. It was all her fault.

"I'm poison." She hiccuped and wiped her eyes with the tissue the woman had handed her.

"Oh, don't be silly," she said. "You're no such thing. It was fate." She nodded and her eyes narrowed. "Just look at me." She motioned with her hands. There were wires coming out of her left arm, but the woman didn't seem to mind. "Do you know why I'm here?"

Alex shook her head and dried her eyes.

"You wouldn't think to look at me, but I'll be one hundred tomorrow and I can tell you, I never thought I'd make it this far." She smiled a little, sadness in her eyes. "I've outlived three husbands, two children, two grandchildren and even a great-grandson who died during birth. I'm ready and happy to go home. Everything that put me here or took my sweet babies away was meant to be. You've been through some rough patches, and your man will make it through this." She nodded. "Just wait and see. You'll both be stronger for it." She tilted her head and looked at her. "Sometimes things like this happen in order to change the direction you were heading." She sighed and leaned back on her pillow. "You wait and see. You and your Grant will look back at this day and remember it as the day everything changed." She sighed and closed her eyes.

Alex sat there in the darkening room, listening to the old woman breathe as she slept. She didn't know her name or if she was right. She only knew that she couldn't stand to walk out the door and find out what was going on. She was scared that the news was bad and the longer she sat in hiding, the longer she could make believe that Grant was okay. That he was out of surgery and that everything was going to be alright.

Finally, when a nurse came in, she quietly excused herself and went to find her family. When she asked the main desk for directions, the nurse smiled. "Your family has been looking for you." The woman stood up. "Come on, honey, I'll take you to them."

She hadn't asked about Grant. She couldn't stand to know if she'd lost him. Her mind had played so many scenarios in the last couple hours and none of them had ended up happy. When she walked into the private waiting room, Alex's heart dropped. The look on everyone's faces told her everything she needed to know. Her eyes closed as she swayed and then her whole world changed.

Patty stood at the stove, a smile placed on her perfectly glossed lips. Her apron was in place, and her sleeves were rolled up so that the grease from the chicken didn't splatter on her clothing.

Everything had to be perfect for when Roy and Travis got home. After all, they were the perfect husband and son and they deserved the best.

Flipping a piece of chicken, she watched as the sheriff's car pulled into her driveway and she wondered what Stephen was doing here. Maybe he wanted to stay for dinner, she thought as she turned the heat on the stove down.

Walking over, she greeted him just as Roy's car drove up.

"Well, evening, Sheriff. Would you like to stay for dinner?" she asked as Roy walked up the driveway, a frown on his face.

"No, ma'am. I'm..." He cleared his throat and looked to Roy.

"Patty, he's here to arrest you for shooting Grant Holton. Why'd you do it, Patty?" Roy rushed to her side, taking her hands. She jerked them away. After all, one didn't show emotions publicly; it just wasn't done.

"Really, Roy. It's no big deal." She turned to the sheriff. "This is all some kind of misunderstanding. After all, I did warn them several times that their behavior was unacceptable. They hurt our Travis. It's all their fault that he won't get out of bed, and everyone in town knows that that West girl was no good for our boy. Causing him to drink and get into all that trouble."

She shook her head. "Really, honestly." She wiped her hands on her apron. "I'm surprised someone hadn't done something about it sooner."

"Are you confessing to shooting Grant Holton?" the sheriff asked.

"Well," she frowned at him. "I don't know about confessions, but of course I did." She leaned closer to the sheriff. "Really Stephen, that girl needs to be taught a lesson. One would think she would behave better since God took her mother and father away. But it's apparent the only way she is going to learn is by losing everything she wants. I tried to get onto Saddleback Ranch to teach her some lessons, but Chase and the men there were always around, so..." She shrugged her shoulders. "I decided Grant was the only way to get to her." She shook her head and chuckled.

"Patty Nolan, you're under arrest for the attempted murder of Grant—"

She laughed. "Really, this is all just a misunderstanding. Once I explain everything to you again..." She trailed off as Stephen put handcuffs on her and started pulling her towards his car. When she looked back at her house, Roy was standing there looking at her like he didn't know who she was. But what really hurt was seeing her boy, her one and only son, standing next to his father, looking at her like she was completely crazy.

Jill Sanders

Chapter Seventeen

She woke to the sweetest voice she'd ever heard. The deep sound vibrated in her mind. Keeping her eyes closed, she listened as he called her name over and over again. She must be dreaming…or dead. That thought caused her eyes to jerk open. She looked up into her sister's face and frowned. She'd sworn she'd heard Grant.

"Grant?" She started sitting up.

"He's here." Haley smiled and nodded to the right.

"Alex, my god, don't scare me like that again," Grant said as she looked over at him. He was sitting up in a hospital bed, a white sling on his left shoulder. Thick bandages were wrapped around his bare chest. His tan face was pale and he looked very tired. His hair was a mess, but he was alive.

Alex was up in a rush and by his side. "You're

255

okay?" she asked, running her eyes over every inch of him.

He reached up, touching her face and nodding. "Looks that way."

The room quietly emptied as they looked at each other, tears running down her face. "I thought..." She took a deep breath and tried again as he took her hands with his. "I thought I'd lost you."

He smiled weakly. "Not even close. The doctor said the bullet bounced off my ribs." He chuckled, then held his side and groaned a little. "He asked me how much milk I drank as a kid." He smiled.

She looked down at their joined hands and tried to pull free, but he held on, pulling gently until she sat next to him, their eyes level.

"I'm sorry. Grant, I never thought that anything like this would happen."

"Of course you didn't." He frowned. "I didn't even see it coming. Makes me wonder if it was Patty doing all those other things all along, instead of Travis." He put a finger under her chin and gently pushed until she looked at him again. "There's no way either of us could have seen it coming."

"Yes, but...I could have..." He put his finger over her lips.

"You were there." She watched as a tear slipped down his face. "If you hadn't been, I could have lay there and bled to death until you got home. You saved me." He blinked and tried to pull her closer. She leaned in.

"You saved me," he repeated and placed his lips on hers. The kiss was different than all the rest they had shared. It marked her, branded her. She felt something shift inside her and closed her eyes to it. Then she released what she'd bottled up inside herself for so long, since that day she watched her mother die. Opening her eyes and pulling back, she took his face in her hands and smiled. "She was right." She smiled.

"Who?" He smiled back at her.

"The old woman. This has changed everything."

His eyebrows shot up in question.

"Grant, I don't want to live with you." She saw his instant frown and chuckled. "I want to marry you. I love you. I love you for your kindness, for your honesty, for the way you are with people and animals. There are so many reasons why." She chuckled. "It could take a lifetime to go through them all. Tell me you'll spend a lifetime with me hearing all of my reasons."

He smiled. "I thought you'd never ask." He pulled her in with his good arm and kissed her again.

Two days later, Grant walked into his house with the help of Alex. They were greeted by Chase, Lauren, Haley, and Grant's parents. Everyone was sitting in the living room, smiling as they watched them walk in slowly.

"I hope you don't mind, I've been staying over here watching over the animals," Chase said, then nodded towards the dog bed by the fireplace.

When they walked in, the small dog's tail started wagging.

"Hey, Junior." He smiled at the small animal whose back half was completely covered in thick white bandages. "How's he doing?" he asked as Alex helped him sit on the couch.

Chase walked over and sat across from them. "He'll live. Might take him some time to get back to puppy mode, and he'll probably have a limp. But he made it through it, which is always a good sign."

The little dog lay his head down again and closed his eyes.

"Patty confessed," his mother broke in, gaining everyone's attention. "Tell them, Glenn." She grabbed his hand.

His dad nodded. "Yes, well. She's confessed and

258

is pleading insanity." His father frowned. "She owned up to everything that's happened over the last couple months. Even the attack on Alex at the rodeo."

"Why?" Alex asked, taking Grant's hand in hers. She felt herself shaking as he ran his fingers over her palms.

Glenn shook his head. "She claims that she just wanted to make her son happy." He nodded to Alex. "So she did everything she could to get back at you and Grant for hurting him, including framing Grant for the attack on you. She talked about how you had shamed their family. How you had destroyed her son and ruined him." He shook his head.

"She said that Travis was happiest when he was with you. So she did everything she could to get Grant out of the way. She was under the assumption that it was you who was pregnant, instead of Lauren. She still won't believe that you're not carrying Travis' baby."

"She must be crazy," Lauren said, walking over and sitting next to Chase. "What's going to happen to her?"

"Well, it will be up to the courts now. If they find her guilty of attempted murder, she'll get anywhere from two to twenty years. If they find her criminally insane, she may get as little as a year in an institution."

"What?" Lauren sat forward, anger flashing in

her eyes. Chase reached over and took her arm. "It's up to the courts." He patted her arm and everyone could see her relax a little.

"What about the mayor?" Alex asked Grant's parents.

Glenn shook his head. "He knew nothing about what his wife had been doing. He's stepping down as mayor. It'll be official tomorrow. There will be an emergency city council meeting next week to decide who will cover until the next election season."

"Travis?" Alex asked next.

Glenn shook his head again. "He left town shortly after they arrested his mother. He was shocked and embarrassed."

Alex sighed and rested back against Grant's good shoulder. He wrapped his arm around her and held on tight. She felt good in his arms. She felt right.

By the time everyone left the house, Grant was tired. The two broken ribs weighed heavily and slowed him down. Not to mention the stitches that held his hide back together. He was stiff and sore all over. Even his knees hurt.

Alex cooed over Junior until finally she carried him back into their bedroom, lying his bed down on her side of the room so she could watch over him.

"You know," he said, as she lay down next to

him. "The doctor said if the bullet hadn't been slowed down by him"—he nodded to the sleeping puppy—"that it might have completely penetrated my ribs and struck a vital organ. So, in a way," he smiled, "you both saved me."

She smiled and leaned closer to him, placing a soft kiss on his lips. "I guess we both owe Junior a lot."

His grin doubled.

"What?" she asked, pulling back a little.

"You called him Junior." He smiled, knowing he'd won everything he'd ever wanted.

Jill Sanders

Epilogue

Alex stood next to the glass and watched the nurse lay down the baby. Its shiny bald head was the cutest thing she'd ever seen. How could she be in love so quickly? She smiled and waved as the little boy's eyes blinked frantically as the nurse cleaned him.

"Isn't he beautiful?" she asked Grant, who was standing next to her.

"He's a keeper." Grant leaned against the glass and looked at her, then sighed.

"What?" She quickly looked away from her nephew for a second to give her husband of three months a glance.

"Just looking at the prettiest girl in Texas." He smiled.

"Grant Holton." She turned and crossed her arms over her chest. "What do you want now?"

His smile was fast. "Kids," he said, simply. "Like that one. A girl would do nicely, too." He crossed his arms over his chest. His stance screamed cowboy even though his clothes yelled lawyer at the moment.

She smiled slowly at him. "Really? Just how soon are you thinking you'll want one of those?"

"One?" He frowned a little. "If you remember correctly, I said 'kids,' as in plural."

She stepped closer and wrapped her arms around his neck. "Oh, I heard you, alright. How many are we talking?"

"Well…" He reached up and scratched his chin and smiled. "Since we have four extra bedrooms, I was thinking that number was good."

She smiled. "How soon are you thinking of starting this family, Counselor?"

"Soon." He leaned down and placed a soft kiss on her lips. She pulled his head down, deepening it until they were both breathless. "We could always start now…" He smiled and started to pull her down the hallway.

"Oh, no. We can't take this special moment away from Lauren and Chase. Besides, I'm dying to know what they are going to name my nephew."

"Fine." He rolled his eyes, then leaned in for another long, slow kiss. "Let's go see what the little tyke's name is."

"God," she said, taking his arm, "I hope they didn't name him something dumb."

When they walked back into Lauren's private hospital room, everyone was there. Haley sat in the corner, talking to Chase's new stepmother, Charlotte. Chase was talking to his father near the window.

"Well, he's getting his first bath and screaming his head off while he's at it," Alex said, walking in and sitting gently by her sister. "Are you ready to

264

tell us all what you've named him yet?"

Chase walked over and sat on the other side of Lauren, taking her hand. They smiled at each other.

"We decided to name him after the man who raised a bunch of rowdy cowgirls all by himself," Lauren said, smiling. "Richard Chase Graham."

Holding Haley

Haley has waited her whole life for Wes. They were secret sweethearts all throughout school, but when he shocks her by joining the military fresh out of school, she's heartbroken and left to wait until the day he comes home. But it's been five long years and she has finally decided to move on with her life. That is until he walks back into town, sexier than ever.

Wes has had one thing on his mind since leaving town: getting back to Haley. Seeing and experiencing what he did oversees has made him realize what he almost let slip through his fingers. All he wants now is to prove to her that waiting for him was the right choice.

About the Author

Jill Sanders is the New York Times and USA Today bestselling author of the Pride Series, the Secret Series, and the West Series romance novels. Having sold over 150,000 books within six months of her first release, she continues to lure new readers with her sweet and sexy stories. Her books are available in every English-speaking country and are now being translated into six different languages and recorded for audiobook.

Born as an identical twin to a large family, she was raised in the Pacific Northwest. She later relocated to Colorado for college and a successful IT career before discovering her talent as a writer. She now makes her home in charming rural Texas where she enjoys hiking, swimming, wine tasting, and, of course, writing.

Made in the USA
Lexington, KY
15 March 2015